PiCKLE
IMPOSSiBLE

PICKLE IMPOSSIBLE

Eli Stutz

illustrations by C.B. Canga

BLOOMSBURY

NEW YORK BERLIN LONDON

First published in the United States of America in June 2010
by Bloomsbury Books for Young Readers
www.bloomsburykids.com

For information about permission to reproduce selections
from this book, write to Permissions, Bloomsbury BFYR,
175 Fifth Avenue, New York, New York 10010

Library of Congress Cataloging-in-Publication Data
Stutz, Eli.
Pickle impossible / by Eli Stutz. — 1st U.S. ed.
          p.   cm.
Summary: Pierre, a particularly average French boy, and Aurore,
the granddaughter of a family enemy, are pursued by would-be thieves
as they try to get a jar of pickles to Bern, Switzerland, to enter
a contest in hopes of saving Pierre's family farm.
ISBN 978-1-59990-464-1
[1. Adventure and adventurers—Fiction. 2. Robbers and outlaws—Fiction.
3. Pickles—Fiction. 4. Contests—Fiction.] I. Title.
PZ7.S9418Pic 2010   [Fic]—dc22   2009035313

Book design by Donna Mark
Typeset by Westchester Book Composition
Printed in the U.S.A. by Worldcolor Fairfield, Pennsylvania
2 4 6 8 10 9 7 5 3 1

For Tziona, Shoham,
Shalhevet, and Naftali

PICKLE
IMPOSSIBLE

PROLOGUE

Somebody Is Watching . . .

The boy set his head down and waited for the gun to go off.

Bang!

With a jolt, he launched himself down the track, pumping his arms back and forth, moving his legs as fast as they would go.

He was aware of the other boys on his left and right—he was in the middle lane, as usual.

Just this once, let it be different, he said to himself. *Just this once.*

The dust flew from his feet. The wind rushed past his face. He forced himself to go faster.

The finish line came into view.

There were cheers erupting from the stands—the other grades, on recess, were watching. Were they cheering him?

As the white tape approached, he clearly saw two of the other runners pull ahead of him. His chest hurt. He gave one last push.

The tape broke.

The race was over. The crowd was on its feet. But not for him.

He was a few steps behind. As always.

The gym teacher walked over to tell each of the runners their times.

He knew what he would hear before he was told.

"14.25 seconds, Pierre, exactly the class average. Good try."

The boy collapsed on the earth, breathing hard.

Each time it was the same.

But far off, past the stands, just over the fence and behind a hedge, a girl was watching. She lowered her high-powered surveillance camera and spoke into a walkie-talkie.

"He doesn't look like much of a threat, Grandfather. Do you want me to keep following him?"

"That won't be necessary, my dear. Pierre La Bouche will never amount to anything. He's a *cornichon*—a good-for-nothing. Move on to the others. Over and out."

The girl switched off her walkie-talkie. She picked up her camera again and focused it on the boy. His nearly brown eyes looked up, turned in her direction, and squinted, trying to see something. It was almost as if he could see her.

She lowered the camera quickly and ducked beneath the leaves.

Her grandfather's words echoed in her mind, but still, there was something that bothered her . . . some small doubt. "My grandfather's right, he's just a cornichon," she told herself. "I'd better get moving."

Could a good-for-nothing ever amount to anything?

CHAPTER 1

The Greatest Story of All Time

I'm yanked from my home, then prodded and felt,
Bathed in hot juices that make my skin welt.
Locked in a dungeon and left there to stew,
'Til I'm snatched up and gobbled by someone like you.
What am I?

This is an unbelievable story. But it's true. This is the greatest, most exciting story you'll probably read all year, maybe even all of your life. And the best thing about it is that I'm the star. My name is Aurore. That means "first light," so I guess the name fits!

Today I'm a simple twelve-year-old French farm

girl. But by this time next year, I'll be a famous actress. So remember that name—Aurore. I'm sure that by the time you finish this book, you won't be able to forget it.

Have you figured out the riddle on the previous page? Can you guess who the girl with the camera was? This story is full of mysteries, so I think I'll leave you guessing for now.

Just so you know, this book isn't only about pickles. It's about something extraordinarily fabulous that happened to me—well, to me and to my friend Pierre. You see, we've just had an incredible adventure, across continents, over land, sea, and air, battling criminals of the worst kind, and trying to win . . . oh, dear . . . I shouldn't give away too much—otherwise you won't read this story, and I won't become a famous actress.

But first you must be wondering why I am writing this story in English. Well, there is no more patriotic person than myself. And I love my dear homeland, France. (*Vive la France!* Long live France!) But to become a movie star, my secret plan is to write a famous book in English, because English is the language of America, and in America some Hollywood producer will decide that this book simply must be made into a movie. And then, because he'll see my picture on the jacket and realize that I'm not only a great storyteller and a heroine but also a beautiful and striking young lady, he'll call me up and ask if I would do him the honor of starring in a movie based on this book. (Of course, the part of Pierre—whom you'll get to know soon— will have to be played by a genuine Hollywood actor—you see, the real Pierre is just average at acting, and his looks are just, well, average.) So then I'll say that I'd love to star in the movie, and everyone will see it, and I'll win an Oscar for Best Actress, and then I'll move to America, and then I'll be . . . ah, wait. I'm not sure about the moving-to-America part. I guess we'll deal with that later.

I should warn you that not everything in this story is nice. In fact, some of it is extraordinarily strange. Some of it I don't even understand myself. But don't worry, things turn out okay—mostly. I wouldn't be here to tell the story if they didn't.

Ah, the story. You must be getting impatient. Well, enough about myself. Let us begin the greatest adventure of all time. Fasten your seat belts, reader, and ready yourself to be blown away. It all starts with . . . a jar of pickles.

CHAPTER 2

Who Will Go?

"This is the best jar of pickles I have ever made," declared Grandfather Henri La Bouche.

The sun had already gone down on the farm. The La Bouche family was sitting around the kitchen table, in the middle of which stood a very plain-looking jar of pickles.

Everyone looked up and stared at the jar:

Marc La Bouche, the father, was still nibbling on dessert—a croissant, but not a cheese one, of course.

Frieda La Bouche, the mother, was tackling her third cup of coffee, trying to fight off a bout of sleep.

Chantal La Bouche, the older sister, was brushing a particle of dust off her sleeve.

Under the table, little Jo Jo La Bouche was busy tying his brother Pierre's shoelaces together, something he did almost every day.

And Pierre La Bouche? He was sitting quietly, in the middle of this meeting, wondering what all the fuss was about.

"Our farm is in trouble," said Grandfather Henri quietly, almost in a whisper. Henri was thin and had wispy gray hair, but fierce blue eyes. His mouth, which was now closed, bulged out strangely at the cheeks.

As he spoke, his voice grew stronger. "For years we have just scraped by, making the finest pickles and selling them in the local markets. The cornichon, the tiny French cucumber, is, as you know, not only a local delicacy when pickled, but also the crowning joy of many great French dishes. *Raclette*, for example—"

At the word "raclette" (which is a dish made of pickles, cheese, and all sorts of other delicious things), Marc began to choke on his croissant. Marc La Bouche was a balding man with a potbelly, and he was almost always relaxed. But now his relaxed demeanor disappeared, and a look of fear and dismay came over his face. "P-p-please, d-d-don't mention anything that has ch-ch-ch- . . . ch-ch-ch- . . . ch-ch-ch-cheeese in it."

"I am sorry, my son," apologized Henri. "I had momentarily forgotten." Marc's face relaxed almost as quickly as it had tensed up.

"Our situation is desperate," said Henri, laying his hands on the table. "If we cannot somehow raise or find $100,000 in the next month, then the La Bouche farm will be sold."

Marc breathed a sigh of resignation. Chantal rubbed her hands nervously. Jo Jo perked his head up from his mischief. Pierre just stared at the jar of pickles.

"There's no way we can come up with that kind of money in a month," said Frieda. "So you mean we're going to have to pack up this whole kit and caboodle, like they say here—toot sweet?" I forgot to mention: Frieda is from Brooklyn, New York, and still speaks like a New Yorker. She is tall and thin and has long, wavy black hair (not as wavy or as pretty as mine, of course, but quite nice in any case).

"I like it here," said Pierre. "I don't want to

leave." It was the first time he had spoken during the meeting.

"Yeah, me too," said Jo Jo, getting up from under the table. "I don't want to leave."

Henri patted Jo Jo's wild, carrot-colored hair. "Of course, Jo Jo," he said. "None of us wants to leave."

Chantal shifted in her chair. "I wouldn't mind," she said quickly, "if it means going somewhere cleaner than this hovel." Chantal had very clean white skin and a long, pointy nose. As she said this, she thrust her hands into her pockets, which were stuffed with her favorite companions—bars of soap.

"Chantal!" scolded Frieda. "Don't talk like that to your grandfather. This farm is no hovel, and we have it great here. My fifteen years here have been the best years of my life." Frieda became weepy and she nuzzled up to Marc, who put his arm around her supportively. Clearly, the majority of the La Bouches did not want to leave.

"But, Father," said Marc, "what can we do? The situation is, as you say, hopeless."

"I said it was desperate. But I did not say that it was hopeless," said Henri mysteriously, gazing into the jar of pickles before him. "There is one hope."

Silence. Everyone waited to hear what Henri would say.

"This jar of pickles is our last hope," he whispered. "In three days' time, a great event will occur. Look!"

Henri cast a piece of paper—a flyer—onto the table. The La Bouches bent over to read it. Here is what it said:

PICKLELYMPICS

THE GRAND INTERNATIONAL PICKLE CONTEST

The Best Pickle of a Decade Will Be
Chosen by World Pickle Experts

Wednesday, July 15
Graubünden Hall
Bern, Switzerland

THE GOLD MEDAL WINNER WILL RECEIVE A CASH PRIZE OF $100,000

Deadline for submission of your jar:
precisely twelve noon on the day of the contest

The family was speechless. Henri looked from face to face.

"This is our chance, my loved ones," he said. "I have poured every last ounce of my talent and my years of experience into this jar of pickles. I am confident that it is the best jar of pickles I have ever made, and it may well be the best jar of pickles in the world. If we win this contest, we can hold on to this farm. Now—which of you will go?"

All eyes turned to Marc La Bouche. He was, after all, the father. Marc looked down. "Did you say Switzerland?" he asked timidly. "Don't they have a lot of ch-ch-ch-ch . . . ch-ch-ch-ch . . . ."

"Cheese?" little Jo Jo blurted out. Marc hid his head under his large hands.

"Yes," said Grandfather Henri, "I'm afraid there may be some of that in Switzerland."

Marc peeked out from under his fingers. "Then I don't think I can go," he said quietly.

They looked at Chantal.

"Don't look at me," she said. "I'm not going to travel to Switzerland on some grimy train, to some grimy contest hall, in some grimy city that is famous for its bear pits. What if the seats at the contest aren't clean? What if I have to use a public bathroom?"

"I'll go!" cried Jo Jo, jumping up, his green eyes twinkling. "Can I, can I?" he said, prodding his mother. Everyone looked at Frieda. But she was fast asleep, her nose smack in the middle of her third cup of coffee. I should explain that Frieda is a sleepaholic.

"You are a wonderful boy, Jo Jo," said Henri, smiling, "but I am afraid that you cannot go—you are too young. Besides, there will probably be balloons there—it is a festive contest, and they would only distract you. And your mother cannot go either—she might sleep straight through the contest, miss a train, or, worse yet, fall asleep on the train and end up who knows where. You don't need me to tell you the story of how your mother ended up on this farm."

Marc sighed. "Well, then, who can we send? What about you, Father?"

For the first time, Henri looked flustered. He actually turned bright red. "Me?" he asked. And then under his breath, in a low voice: "Who knows? *She* might be there . . ." He quickly turned back to

Marc and said, "My son, I can't very well go to a public contest with the way I look."

Pierre raised his head. *Strange*, he thought. *Grandfather has never worried about his looks before. I wonder . . .*

"Don't tell us you're embarrassed about your mouth, Grandfather," said Chantal. "Some very famous people have a marble mouth, and it doesn't stop them from going out in public."

It was true—it really could be said that Henri had a marble mouth, ever since that incident in the trenches (that comes up later in the story). What is a marble mouth? Suffice it to say, he had enormous bulges in his lower cheeks that looked like he was trying to hold at least a dozen large marbles in his mouth.

Henri heaved his shoulders. He looked beaten. "I confess," he said. "I am quite afraid I would be laughed at . . . I cannot go."

And Pierre thought, *There must be a different reason.*

"Well, then, that's it," said Chantal. "None of us can go. The farm is lost, and maybe we'll move to an apartment building in Paris and start a new life. I say good riddance."

The rest of them looked glum. Frieda woke up. Slowly, each of the family members got up from the table and started to walk away.

Except for Jo Jo. He had just finished popping the bubbles in his mother's coffee cup, which had emerged when she breathed out through her nose and into the black swirling liquid (popping bubbles and balloons was Jo Jo's favorite hobby). "What about Pierre?" said Jo Jo.

Henri swiveled around like a man half his age. His gaze lit on Pierre, who was trying to get up inconspicuously, hoping that nobody would mention his name.

"That's it, Jo Jo!" he cried, jumping up and down. "Pierre will go!"

Marc walked over to Pierre and tousled his son's hair (which, like his eyes, was a color closest to but not quite brown). "Father, Pierre is no cross-country traveler. Why, he's never been farther than Paris, and that was with the whole family last year."

Chantal snickered. "I wouldn't trust Pierre to deliver the mail to the neighbors. He's not a very bright boy. How do you know he won't get lost or lose the pickles?"

At that, Pierre reddened. He knew it all too well. He really was a very simple boy—he had never excelled at anything. At school, kids called him "the cornichon," which, besides meaning "pickle," also happens to be a nickname in France for people who aren't very successful.

"No!" cried Henri excitedly. "Pierre is the perfect choice. He is not too fast and not too slow. He is not too strong and not too weak. He's not a genius, but also not a dunce. We don't need a hero. Just a regular, normal, average messenger to take a jar of pickles to a contest. Yes! Pierre is normal. Pierre is average. Pierre is the perfect man for our job!" Henri turned to Pierre. "Will you take the jar of pickles to the contest?"

"Okay," said Pierre simply.

"Wonderful!" shouted Henri. "Here, Pierre, take the jar!"

Pierre got up to take the jar. He tripped, falling flat on his face. Jo Jo burst out laughing, pointing at the tied shoelaces.

It worked every time.

CHAPTER 3

An Unexpectedly Short Train Ride

I realized something you might be wondering about when you read this story: how on earth do I know all the things that happened in the adventure? Especially the beginning parts about what happened to Pierre before I landed on the scene? Well, I may say that you are a very smart boy or girl to be asking such a brilliant question. It shows that you are very intelligent and should excel in life and go to university and maybe even become a famous professor. The answer to your ingenious question is that after the adventure had ended, I did interviews with Pierre and his family members about everything that happened and asked them a lot of questions, and they filled me in on all the missing parts. And that's how I know how the whole story fits together. So this means that not only am I a heroine, but I'm also an amazing investigator, and if somehow my acting career does not pan out, then at least I'll be able to fall back on being the best detective in France or maybe even all of Europe.

"*Au revoir*, Pierre!" called Frieda from the platform as the train pulled out of the station. "Good-bye and good luck! We'll miss you!"

Pierre waved from the window, watching his mother fade into the distance. She had driven him to the train station in the family farm truck. Just before she was out of sight, it seemed to him that she had fallen asleep in a standing position—something only she could do.

Pierre had two things in his hands: the jar of pickles, and a small blue envelope his mother had given him as she kissed him good-bye. "Don't open this envelope unless you're in a *real* jam," she had said to him. Pierre had put the envelope in his pants pocket.

The old-fashioned little train picked up speed as it left Châteaubriant, the small town that was closest to the La Bouche farm. The plan was for Pierre to travel on this train to a larger town called Le Mans, and from there to Paris. In Paris, Pierre would board a modern high-speed train and zoom off on a four-and-a-half-hour journey to Bern, Switzerland, where the pickle contest was to take place.

Rolling farmlands and the odd tree passed by Pierre as he gazed out of the window.

Later, I asked Pierre what he was thinking as he left his home alone for the first time in his life. Here is what he said to me:

"I was watching the trees go by."

"Did you think you would succeed on your mission?" I asked him.

"Not really."

That is how Pierre speaks. He never says too much, only exactly what he needs to say. Sometimes I wonder if he is thinking more than he speaks. That is why it's better that I am writing down this story.

If Pierre wrote it down, it would be about three pages long, no more.

Pierre settled into his seat, still clutching the jar of pickles his grandfather had given him that morning. Pierre thought about his grandfather's last words:

"Whatever you do, Pierre, do not let go of the jar. The jar is everything. When you are awake, make sure it is always on your body. When you sleep, use it as a pillow. Do not let anyone take it from you, or even touch it. Never let it out of your sight. You must protect the jar at all costs."

At that point, Henri La Bouche's face had darkened. *"And beware of the name Borsht."*

"Who is Borsht?" Pierre had asked.

"My worst enemy," his grandfather had said. *"Zacharie Borsht is a rival pickle farmer. He hates me and he will do anything to ruin our chances of winning the contest. He wants our farm for himself."*

"Borsht," said Pierre to himself. Pierre decided to take his grandfather's words to heart. Unstrapping his belt, he widened it to its greatest length and strapped the jar of pickles against his stomach. Then he placed his shirt over the jar so that all anyone would see was a large bulge.

"When I need to sleep, I will use it as a pillow, just as Grandfather said," murmured Pierre.

As he said this, the train entered a tunnel. Suddenly, it became quite dark in Pierre's car, since it was daytime and the cabin lights were off. It was a long tunnel. It had once been the site of the old Grimoire mine, closed ages ago after too many peculiar accidents.

Pierre looked around apprehensively. He was not afraid of the dark, not any more than any other boy. But it seemed to him that there was something different about this cold blackness. "You're just scared because it's your first time away from home alone," he said to himself.

And then he began to hear something.

At first, it was the rumble of the train moving through the tunnel. A kind of low, moaning noise, like the sound you hear when you put a seashell to your ear—the roar of the ocean. But this was deeper, lower. And then, as Pierre sat there riding through that pitch darkness, it seemed he could hear a voice underneath the low, moaning rumble. A gravelly, rocky voice that rose and fell. He could almost make out words . . .

Mmmmmm . . . I wannntttt theemmmmm . . .

Pierre started. Had he really heard that? Who was talking? Were they speaking to him? He tried to ignore the thought. And then he heard it again—

I wannntttt theemmmmm . . . soooo yummmyyyy . . .

What would somebody want from me? Something yummy? Pierre wondered.

He thought he knew.

Mmmmm . . . saaallltttyyy . . . sweeeeett . . . givvve themmm tooo meeee . . .

Pierre clutched the jar of pickles to his chest and closed his eyes. "This can't be happening. It's just your imagination," he said to himself. He had heard of mischievous spirits that haunted deserted mines, but he never really believed those stories could be true. Yet try as he might, he could not shake the feeling that he was being talked to by . . . something.

A few seconds passed by. The voice seemed to have stopped. Pierre breathed a sigh of relief.

Mmmm . . . huuunngggryyy . . . givvve tthheem too meeee . . .

There it was again! And it wanted his pickles!

Suddenly Pierre thought he knew who "it" was. "The tunnel!" he whispered.

Yaahaaahaaa haaahaaa . . . feeeeeedd meeeee!

Pierre had a crazy, wild urge to open the window of the cabin and throw the jar of pickles into the tunnel. But those pickles were his mission. To throw them away would be to abandon his family. And he could not abandon his family.

"No. I won't give them up," said Pierre, gritting his teeth and clutching the jar tightly. "You can't have them!" he said, louder. As he said this, he suddenly felt braver than he had ever felt before.

. . . Givvve ttthheemmm toooo meeee . . .

There was an ugly pause. Pierre braced himself.

. . . Nnnowwwww!

Pierre suddenly felt the tunnel itself quiver ever so slightly, a shake just heavier than the rattling of the train. A large, old, golden coin must have dislodged itself from the rock ceiling of the tunnel, falling onto the track several feet ahead of the train, balancing itself on the left rail. (I know this because the conductor, who was watching the track, reported later in a local paper that he had seen something shiny fall onto the track in the beam of the train's headlight.)

When a train wheel hits something hard on the track, what happens next hangs by a fine thread of balance—a train might go right over it unharmed, or be flipped, all depending on the smallest fraction of a difference in weight to one side or another.

A tense moment passed. Pierre felt something dreadful was about to happen.

The train's front wheel hit the coin. Pierre felt the train jerk rightward, its left wheels lifting clear off the track!

Not knowing why he did this, Pierre very suddenly threw himself to the left. His body thudded against the inner wall of the train, nearly shattering the pickle jar. Pierre's body was a tiny weight compared to the train itself, but as I said, these things hang on the tiniest fraction of balance.

Pierre held himself plastered to the left wall. After an excruciating second, he felt the train right itself and touch down. The gold coin bent, shot off the track, and ricocheted down the tunnel wall. The train continued on its way. Pierre could have sworn he heard a disappointed sigh from the tunnel:

Oooohhhhhhh . . .

The train emerged from the dark tunnel and into the light. Sunlight flooded the cabin. Pierre blinked. Whatever had happened was over. But had it happened altogether? Now in the light of day, Pierre couldn't be so sure. Maybe in his fear, combined with the rumbling of the train, he had imagined it all. Still, he had a distinct feeling that something had happened inside that tunnel *to him*, and that for whatever reason, the Pierre after the tunnel wasn't quite the same person as the Pierre before it.

The train stopped at the next station. A few passengers disembarked, and several others boarded. Pierre glanced self-consciously at his bulging pickle-jar stomach and hoped no one would enter his car. What would they think of him? Would they say anything? The door to his car opened. Pierre looked away at the window, pretending to be absorbed in thought.

"Are you pregnant?" said a voice. It was me! That's right, the Great Aurore, with my biting sense of humor. Yes, this is where I splash onto the scene. I entered the car and sat down opposite Pierre. And that was the first thing I ever said to him. He really did look quite pregnant with that jar of pickles under his shirt.

Pierre's jaw dropped. Of course, it was only natural. I am dazzlingly good-looking, even for a twelve-year-old. And I dress absolutely charmingly, with what clothes a simple farm girl can buy. My hair is gorgeous (have I mentioned that already?)—it's a light auburn color, and it's beautifully long and wavy. And my eyes are deep sea blue.

"No—no," Pierre managed to say.

I gestured toward Pierre's stomach. "Then what is that you are hiding under your shirt?"

"Nothing," said Pierre, trying to recover himself.

"Well, in that case you have a very large belly button," I said, to put him in his place. "What is your name, Mr. Large Belly Button?"

Pierre was turning a nice shade of red. "Pierre," he said.

"Pierre *what*?" I asked.

"Pierre La Bouche," he said.

"Pleased to meet you," I said, putting out my hand. "My name is Aurore and I'm going to Paris for the French national chocolate competition. And since my chocolates are the best, I'm naturally going to win. Here, look." I produced an exquisite wooden box from my bag and proceeded to open it in front of Pierre. I could see his mouth begin to water.

"These are pralines. These are filled with the

finest caramel. And these round ones with the swirl on top are of the purest fudge," I said, pointing to various specimens from my box.

What I did not realize at the time was that while Pierre was born in the very middle of the night, exactly three years and a quarter after Chantal and exactly three years and a quarter before Jo Jo, at the stroke of midnight of the spring equinox (which is exactly in the middle between the summer and winter solstices), in the middle of a taxi-cab, which was stuck in the middle of a traffic jam on a midsized road that was precisely equidistant between the hospitals of Le Mans and Paris, and that Pierre's hair, when it grew, split into two clumps down the very middle of his head, and that every single test he took at school he scored exactly the average class score, and that every race he ran at gym he finished precisely in the middle place, and, well, I could go on forever . . . the point is, that while Pierre was always exactly in the middle of every situation in every way, there was one exception, and that was his extraordinary love and weakness for chocolate.

"May I try one?" asked Pierre, trying to sound casual.

I stifled a smile. "I'll give you one if you show me what you're hiding."

That made him think. He was silent for a moment. Then he looked out the window, considering. He kept shooting furtive glances at the chocolates. *Why would I endanger my whole mission over a silly piece of chocolate?* he asked himself. And yet, they looked so tempting . . .

A minute passed. "Well?" I asked. "Are you going to show me what it is?"

Pierre just kept on looking out the window. He was visibly salivating.

Another minute of excruciating torture passed. Pierre couldn't take it any longer. "Okay," he said finally, raising his shirt and showing me the jar of pickles.

"A jar of pickles?" I said. "That's your big secret? What's so special about it?"

"I'm taking them to a contest," said Pierre. "In Switzerland."

"I see," I said. "Well, I suppose that is special. Now, for showing your secret to me, you get to pick a chocolate." I held out the box so that he could pick. "Just one. I have to save the rest for the competition."

Pierre licked his lips. He was having difficulty choosing. At last he selected the fudge swirl. He put it into his mouth and chewed, his eyes closing for a moment in pure pleasure.

"This is very good," he said after he had swallowed.

"Of course it's good," I said. "It's the best. And with it, I will win the grand prize of the competition."

"What's the grand prize?" asked Pierre.

I hesitated, watching Pierre. He blinked, shook his head, then blinked again. "The prize?" I asked.

"Yess," said Pierre a bit slowly, and with a slur in his voice. He put his hand to his head. "The prrrizzzze ..." His eyes were blinking, and then closing ...

"The prize," I said again, as Pierre lost consciousness and fell to his side, "is your jar of pickles."

CHAPTER 4

The Wet Prisoner

Did I mention that I am an excellent actress? Well, I guess I didn't have to be that excellent to entrap Pierre. He was never especially watchful. But I may have told you that I always tell the truth. I suppose that is not entirely true. I have been known to twist a word or two here and there. Perhaps we can call it pretending to be something I am not. I sometimes like the phrase "white lie." Was I traveling to a chocolate competition in Paris? Not exactly. Well, not really at all. Did I meet Pierre entirely by accident? Did I not already know his name and what he was carrying with him before I entered his train car?

You are probably already guessing the answers to those questions. Do you now know who was spying on Pierre in the schoolyard?

Well, this really is somewhat embarrassing. Okay—I admit it—I did something very, very bad. I spied on and fooled an innocent boy, medicated him to sleep, and then handed him over to . . . well, we'll get to that soon. But hold on! Before you condemn me in your heart as a criminal, let me assure you that I have made up for my crime. That's right—I am not the evil enemy of this book, only a relative of his. And I sincerely promise not to mislead you, the reader, again. From here onward, every word you will read is the plain and simple truth. I hope I have convinced you. And if I have not . . . well, you will see . . . In any case, let us return to Pierre.

Pierre woke up. His head hurt. He opened his eyes. It wasn't much better than when they were closed. It was absolutely dark. *Bump—bump—*

bumpety—bump. "I must be in a car," he said to himself. He was lying down. He tried to move his hands—no good; they were tied behind his back. His legs too were tied. *The pickles!* thought Pierre. He jiggled around, rolling this way and that. He could not feel the precious jar! *Oh, what has happened to me!* he thought. *That girl, Aurore! She gave me a chocolate, and then, and then—I can't remember. Oh, think, Pierre! Why would you have fallen asleep and then ended up in the trunk of a car?* The wheels in Pierre's mind began to turn. *That's it,* he thought. *The chocolate must have had a sleeping potion. Oh, you fool. She wanted to steal those pickles, and now look where you are. You have failed in your mission. The farm will be sold and it's all your fault.* Pierre began to cry at the thought of it.

After a few minutes of bumping around in the trunk, Pierre felt the car come to a stop. The trunk opened. Four rough hands seized Pierre and carried him out into the dim light of a barn. Pierre blinked, looking at his captors.

"He doesn't look like anything special," said the first, a huge, burly man with hair on his chest and arms. He had a dark, tangled beard.

"Never mind how the little cornichon looks," said a short, thin man with flaky blond hair. He had delicate spectacles perched on his nose. "The main point is that Monsieur Borsht has what he came for."

Monsieur Borsht! thought Pierre. *That's the man Grandfather told me to watch out for. And now he's got me—and he has the pickles too!*

"What do we do with him now?" asked the huge man.

"Monsieur Borsht said that he must spend the night here," said the thin man. The huge man grasped Pierre and carried him over to a corner. He set him down roughly on a pile of hay. "There you are, my little *garçon*. I am sorry about your accommodations, but at least you have a soft bed, ha, ha!"

"What are you going to do with me?" Pierre had the courage to ask.

The thin man walked over and looked at Pierre with beady eyes from over his spectacles. "You are a prisoner, boy. But if you behave well, then perhaps the master will let you go. If not, I warn you that your life would be in peril!"

The men started to walk away.

That was when Pierre noticed that he was very thirsty. "Wait," he said. "Can I please have a drink of water?"

The huge man began to walk toward a faucet on the wall.

"Stop that!" said the thin man. "You can wait until tomorrow morning, prisoner. I guarantee we'll bring you a fine breakfast." With that, he sneered, and the two of them left the barn, shutting the large door behind them. Pierre could hear a *chink* from the other side of it—the sound of a lock being turned.

When they had opened and closed the barn door, Pierre had glimpsed the sky outside. It was dark navy blue. A ray of moonlight shot through a small hole in the roof. It was definitely nighttime.

"Well, at least this is better than being in the trunk of that car," he said to himself. "But I wish I could get a drink."

Pierre rolled off the hay and toward the faucet on the wall. He looked up at it. A drop of water fell from it and landed on his forehead. *With my hands and feet tied, there's no way I can turn it on,* he thought. He moved his head upward slightly. The next drop fell into his mouth. *This is no good either,* he thought.

How much water can I get from a drop here and a drop there?

Then Pierre had an idea. He bent his legs until they were under his body, then straightened them, so that he was in a kneeling position. He rubbed his cheek against the faucet—it did not move. Then he put his mouth around it, and bit down on it with his teeth. At the same time, he twisted his head counter-clockwise. Suddenly the water turned on at full blast, quickly soaking Pierre's neck, shirt, and pants before he could wrench himself away. "Ugghh," he groaned. He was still thirsty, so he tried to put his mouth into the gushing flow. It was quite a shock, but at least he got a good drink out of it. When he was done, he put his teeth back onto the faucet to close it, and pulled. It was no good; the faucet would not turn. It was stuck.

By now Pierre was completely soaked from head to foot, and the water was creating a nice big pool on the floor of the barn. Pierre tried again, but it was no use. He simply couldn't turn off the water. *Oh, well,* he thought. *I guess I'll try to make the best of it.* He rolled over a few times until he was several feet away from the faucet and at the edge of the pile of hay. But try as he might, he could not get up onto the pile. Soon he was lying in a deepening pool of cold water.

"I will be drowned!" Pierre shouted. With his last strength, he heaved his upper body onto the pile and wrenched his legs up after him. This was much better. Now he was out of the pool. "I hope the water doesn't rise to this level," he said to himself. It didn't—rather, it seemed to be draining from under the door of the barn. "Maybe they'll name the river after me," said Pierre. "The Pierre River," he said, chuckling at the sound of it. It was the first time he had laughed in a long while. Somehow, the thought comforted him. Then, completely drenched from head to toe, shivering somewhat in the cool night air, Pierre fell asleep. He was exhausted.

At this point you are probably thinking to yourself: "Aurore is the nastiest, cruelest, most coldhearted girl in the universe. How could she kidnap a poor, innocent boy like Pierre and leave him to rot in a filthy barn, soaked to the bone, without food, and with absolutely no hope of escape or freedom?" Well, in that case, you would be right—since that is exactly what I was thinking to myself as I tossed and turned in my normally comfortable farmhouse bed.

I got out of bed and walked over to the mirror. I brushed my fabulous hair and gave myself one of my most dazzling looks. I went to the bathroom and splashed cold water over my perfect face, then went back to my bedroom to read one of my favorite fashion magazines. When I had read it from cover to cover, I smiled to myself, got into bed, and fell fast asleep.

Well, almost. Everything except the sleeping part. It was no good. Try as I might, I could not get Pierre's face out of my head. I shut my eyes tightly. Instead of darkness, I kept seeing the exact split that he had down the middle of his hair. "Why does he have that outrageous split? Why should I care about such a simple boy?" I said to myself. "Why should I risk my neck for someone I hardly know?" I resolved to go to sleep right then and there and to forget about the whole thing.

Which explains why precisely two minutes later, I found myself creeping out of my room, past my grandfather's study (where he was reading the paper), into his private bathroom, and toward his secret medicine cabinet . . .

The farm was cold and silent. A milky white moon gleamed overhead. Pierre snored, then shivered in his sleep, then snored again. Suddenly, he was woken by the sound of the barn lock turning. He looked up through the hole in the roof and saw that it was still nighttime. *What now?* he thought to himself.

The door of the barn opened slowly, and in crept a dark figure. Pierre trembled—what manner of evil was this? The figure spied Pierre and walked over to him. The first thing it did was to produce a small knife, which glinted in the dim light of the barn.

"No, don't hurt me!" said Pierre.

"Shhh . . . ," said the person. "I'm trying to rescue you."

Can you guess who that person was? Who else would have access to the key to the barn? Who else would know where Pierre was being held, and that he was in need? Who else could be as wily and stealthy as a cat burglar if she wanted to, while at the same time be dazzlingly gorgeous and brilliantly witty?

Okay, it was me.

I cut the ropes that tied Pierre's hands and feet, and in a moment he was free.

"Thank you," he said. Then, as I removed my hood, and the light of the barn shone on my elegant features, he exclaimed, "You! How dare you! You tricked me! You—"

I put a gloved hand over his mouth. I did not expect such an outburst from my ordinary Pierre. "Shhh!" I said again.

But Pierre kept flailing his hands about, trying to push me over, so I did the only thing I could do—I swept his feet out from under him with a low roundhouse kick (did I mention I am an adept at jujitsu?). He fell to the floor, in the middle of the pool of water. *Splash!*

He kept on burbling and spluttering, so I reached down and heaved him up onto the hay with both hands. "Why, you're soaked!" I said.

"Of course I'm soaked," said Pierre. Then he began to struggle again, making a lot of noise.

"Stop that!" I said fiercely. "Or we'll both be caught. Now listen, Pierre La Bouche. I'm here to rescue you—do you want my help or not?"

Pierre took one look at me, and then made a dash for the barn door. He got a few feet outside before I tackled him to the ground.

"Will you stop trying to run away from me?" I scolded.

Pierre lifted his head. "Why should I trust you?" he said. "You got me into this mess."

I let go of him and sat down on the grass. "You're right," I said. "You don't have a reason to trust me. But you've got to listen to me. I know where your pickles are."

Pierre looked at me suspiciously. "Who are you?" he asked.

I gave one of my most striking looks. "Aurore," I breathed.

"I know your name," said Pierre. "I mean, who are you really? Why did you kidnap me and why are you helping me now?"

We heard a rustling noise from the direction of the farmhouse.

"There's no time to explain," I said. "But if you

want your pickles back, you've got to come with me now!"

I got up and held out my hand.

Pierre screwed up his face in indecision. He looked behind him, to the farm fence and the road beyond it, and then he looked back at me. *Why should I trust a girl who lied to me?* he thought.

I'd like to imagine that my looks or my winning personality swayed him, but I'm afraid it was something else.

"Take me to the pickles," he said.

CHAPTER 5

Two Wheels to Paris

After we remembered to turn off the barn faucet (that's the Pierre River), I led Pierre to the farmhouse. It was still dark outside. We dashed up to the window of my grandfather's bedroom. I moved a nearby log to the side of the house, and we both climbed up onto it and looked inside.

"Who's that?" whispered Pierre, motioning toward the sleeping man on the bed. The man had flowing silver hair and a pointy gray goatee. Since he was on his back, the goatee pointed straight up. He was snoring.

"That's my grandfather," I told Pierre.

"What is he doing in Monsieur Borsht's house?" asked Pierre.

"My grandfather *is* Monsieur Borsht," I said.

Pierre nearly fell off the log. "That's Monsieur Borsht? You're his granddaughter!" he exclaimed.

"Shhhhh," I whispered. "You're going to wake him up. Look!" My grandfather rolled over in his sleep. As he did this, we could both see a glint of glass under his pillow.

"The pickles!" whispered Pierre. "But how . . . ?"

"Follow me," I said bravely.

I lifted the windowsill up carefully and climbed into the room, quiet as a mouse. Pierre followed, not as quietly, but without any disasters.

We tiptoed over to my grandfather's bed. Beside it, on the bed table, were his sunglasses and a mostly finished glass of wine. The drawer was half open. Inside it, I glimpsed a shiny, black gun-shaped object. Looking closer, I saw an inscription on its side. It read: ZERN ION GUN—Experimental. I knew my grandfather was a weapons enthusiast, but I wondered what this strange addition to his collection could possibly be.

"His eyes are open!" said Pierre, pointing. It was true—my grandfather sleeps with his eyes open. Quite startling, I suppose, for Pierre but not for me.

"No," I reassured him. "He is asleep, see?" I waved my hand back and forth over the open eyes: the real one, and the glass one (more about that later). Pierre relaxed a little.

"The wine of Anjou," I whispered. "It brings such deep dreams."

"You used sleeping medicine on your own grandfather?" asked Pierre with disbelief.

I shrugged.

"You should be a pharmacist," said Pierre.

Well, how else was I supposed to steal back the pickles and rescue Pierre? Don't look at me like that. I promise, this is the last time in this story that I will put somebody to sleep. In any case, I only used the same stuff my grandfather put in the chocolates for Pierre, so he actually got what he deserved. Oh, and let me get something straight. My grandfather *is* the villain of this story, but he's still my grandfather, and while he was never particularly nice to anybody else, he was sometimes considerate of me. In his own way, I think he cared about me. I can't exactly say that I loved him, but I certainly did not hate him either.

"And you are a very impolite boy," I said to Pierre. "Let's just say I have helped him fall asleep. Now for the pickles . . ."

I very gingerly lifted the pillow on which my grandfather's head was resting. He mumbled something in his sleep, and we both froze. But then he resumed snoring, so I snatched the jar of pickles, and let the pillow down gently.

In half a minute we were breathing heavily outside on the grass. I handed Pierre the jar of pickles.

"Thank you," said Pierre, hugging it to his chest. He looked relieved.

"You're welcome," I said. "And I'm sorry about before. Do you forgive me?"

"No," said Pierre.

"Well, then I suppose we can't be friends," I said stiffly.

"I suppose not," said Pierre, shortly. "Well, goodbye, then." Pierre turned and began to walk away. Silly Pierre! Where did he think he was going, wearing soaked clothes, in a strange place far from home with only a jar of pickles?

"Where do you think you are going?" I asked, walking alongside him.

"You know where I'm going," he said.

"The pickle competition in Switzerland?" I said. "But how will you get there?"

"I'll find a way," said Pierre, somewhat unsurely.

"Can I at least give you a lift to Paris?" I said.

"How can *you* give me a lift?" said Pierre.

"I can do a lot of things you'd never guess," I said.

A rooster crowed. The faint glow of morning had lit up the eastern sky. We heard the first sounds of motion from the farmhouse.

"We'd better get out of here," I said. "Come with me." I took Pierre's hand and we ran in the direction of the south gate, which leads to the main road.

But before we reached the gate, the sounds of motion from the farmhouse had become the sounds of a *com*motion, and sharp shouting.

"Zounds! He is gone!" we heard a sharp voice curse.

"The master's not going to like this," said another.

"There they are, you idiot!" said the first voice. And then, "Send the dogs after them—they're nearly at the side gate!"

We heard barking and fierce yelps. Pierre began

to run faster, but I turned around. Two large dogs came bounding up from across the field. "Don't worry!" I said to Pierre. The dogs ran up to me and I began to pet them. "Foofoo, Georgette!" I said. Foofoo and Georgette growled at Pierre, who cringed. "Oh, my little dears, I'm afraid we can't take you with us," I said to them. "Pierre, really, there's nothing to be scared of," I told him. "Good-bye, my sweets," I said. "And do be careful not to wake up Grandfather too early. We need a good head start."

Foofoo and Georgette seemed to understand. They each gave me a lick and bounded off toward the farm, this time not barking.

"But won't your grandfather's men be after us?" said Pierre, breathless.

"Oh, that's already been taken care of," I said, winking.

A moment later, more cursing could be heard from the farm. "The truck—it won't start! *Zut alors!* Somebody's cut the ignition!"

"I was wondering when they would notice that," I said with a laugh. Then I led an openmouthed Pierre into a small shed beside the gate. I cast open the door and flipped on the light switch, revealing a shiny new motorcycle, with two helmets on the seat.

"I almost forgot," I said. "Here, take your bag." I handed Pierre his bag of clothing, which was on the floor beside the motorcycle. A backpack lay beside it—it was mine. I put it on and jumped onto the motorcycle.

"You had this whole thing planned all along," said Pierre.

"I am quite a strategist."

"You think you're something special, don't you?" said Pierre.

"I know I'm something special," I said. With that, I revved up the motorcycle and flooded the motor with gas. *Broom!* it went. "Now don't just stand there, hop on!"

Pierre looked skeptical. "You can drive this thing?"

I raised my eyebrow at Pierre. You should see me when I raise my eyebrow. It is very alarming, and it means, "Don't mess with the Great Aurore."

Pierre got the message. He climbed onto the motorcycle behind me, and we put on our helmets. There were shouts and yells close behind our heels. Through the shed window, Pierre could see my grandfather's henchmen huffing and puffing toward us on foot. "Get back here, you silly kids!" hollered one. I floored the gas. In a flash, we were out of the shed, through the gate, and onto the road.

It was a bumpy road. I sped up and soon the wind was in our hair. Which meant that my hair was in Pierre's face.

"Where are the—*pfff!*—seat belts?" shouted Pierre, trying to spit out tufts of hair.

"There *are* no seat belts!" I shouted back. "Hold on!"

"To what?" shouted Pierre. Oh, Pierre, you can be so simple sometimes.

"To me, you goose!" I said.

Rather than fall, Pierre did the only sensible thing he could do. He held on to me. And we were off, the sounds of pursuit disappearing as we rode into the distance.

At first, the ride went well. I had fun annoying Pierre by singing songs I made up on the spot. Like:

J'aime manger la raclette,
quand je roule sur ma motocyclette.
(I love eating raclette,
when I ride my motorcycle.)

Pierre tried to ignore this (I'm not sure why—my voice is divine), but finally he expressed his annoyance by very casually flicking my ears. I found that infuriating, but since I needed both hands to drive, there was nothing I could do about it but jab him in the ribs from time to time.

This sort of bickering went on nicely for nearly an hour, until we were pulled over by the first policeman who spotted us. He flagged us down from his white patrol car to the side of the road. I probably could have outrun him, but I decided to use my winning personality instead.

"How old are you?" the policeman asked me.

"Seventeen and three-quarters," I exaggerated. Even though I'm twelve, I can surely pass for at least fourteen. I look very mature for my age.

"You expect me to believe that?" asked the policeman. Pierre just looked ahead blankly as if this exchange didn't have to do with him.

"Please, sergeant," I said, "can't you let us go

just this one time? We are really in a very desperate rush."

"Do you have a license to drive this thing?" he asked me.

"Oh, a license?" I smiled, showing all my teeth, and winked. "Did anyone ever tell you that you have a very pretty uniform?"

The policeman was not impressed by my irresistible charm. "I'm afraid I'm going to have to arrest you for driving under the legal age," he said firmly. He took out a notepad. Turning to Pierre, he said, "What's your name, son?" He moved his pen over the page, ready to start jotting down information.

"Pierre La Bouche."

The policeman froze in mid-jot. "Did . . . did you say *La Bouche*?"

"Yes," said Pierre. "Pierre La Bouche."

The policeman's voice trembled very slightly. "Are you related to *Henri La Bouche*?" This exchange was becoming interesting.

"He's my grandfather," said Pierre with a hint of a grin.

The policeman suddenly stood up straight as if he had been shot. His face turned a deep shade of red.

"I apologize for stopping you, *monsieur* and *mademoiselle*," he said. "You can go."

Then he lowered his head and hung his arms at his sides, in a gesture of simultaneous respect and mortification.

Pierre and I were speechless. I was not speechless for long—I rarely am.

"Thank you, kind sir, for your graciousness," I declared, saluting. We zoomed off.

I did not see it, but I now imagine that the policeman just stood there with his hat off, murmuring, "*La Bouche.*"

After the police incident, I decided it best to avoid major towns or cities until we got to Paris. So we veered off onto a side road that would encircle the large town of Le Mans. Neither of us had had anything to eat that morning (and Pierre's last meal was breakfast the day before), so we took a short break. We sat down on the side of the road, under a tree in an empty field.

Going behind a bush, Pierre changed out of his filthy and still-wet clothing and into a fresh set from his bag. When he came back, I had already laid out our breakfast: goat cheese with a baguette and some rose red apples.

"What happened back there with that policeman?" I asked Pierre.

"What do you mean?" said Pierre, wolfing down a piece of baguette and cheese. He was famished.

"I mean, why did he let us go when he heard your name?" I said.

Pierre shrugged. "Maybe he likes Cornichons La Bouche."

A stray cat had come by to watch our meal. He looked mangy and thin, and eager for a morsel.

"That can't be the answer," I said, throwing the cat a small piece of cheese. "No. It was your grandfather's name that did it." I thought for a moment. "What did your grandfather do before he went into the pickle business?"

"I think he was a soldier," said Pierre, biting into an apple, "but that was a long time ago, during the war. He gave up being a soldier when he met my grandmother."

"Is your grandmother still alive?" I asked.

"No," said Pierre, chewing noisily. "She died a

long time ago, before I was born. My grandfather doesn't like to talk about her too much. Anyhow, what does it matter now?"

Pierre can be quite uncivilized sometimes.

"You know it's rude to talk while you are eating," I said, throwing the hungry cat another piece of cheese. "Anyone would think you had learned your manners on a farm."

"And you learned your manners elsewhere?" asked Pierre.

I raised my chin in the air. "I am going to be a very famous personage someday, and I suggest you speak to me with more respect." I gave the cat a piece of my baguette.

"I suggest you stop giving away our food to stray animals," said Pierre.

"Oh, don't be so stingy," I said, petting the grateful cat on the head. "He's half starved."

"Why did you help kidnap me?" said Pierre, changing the topic to something more positive.

"It's simple," I said, lowering my chin half an inch. "My grandfather said he needed my help; he said it was important to him. And . . ."

Pierre narrowed his eyes. "And?"

I looked away. This was embarrassing! "And he

promised to give me this motorcycle as a gift if I said yes."

"Well, then, I see that you don't really care about anyone except for yourself," said Pierre, snatching the last piece of cheese away from the cat.

I frowned. "You are really pushing your luck, Mr. Large Belly Button. It was I who rescued you. And it is I who am helping you get to Paris. What would you do without me?"

Pierre pretended to ignore this very reasonable statement. "What made you decide to rescue me?" he asked. He threw the cat the core of his apple. The cat looked at Pierre curiously, sniffed the core, then turned back to his crumbs of cheese and baguette.

"I—I'm not sure," I said uncertainly (and I am rarely uncertain about anything). "It just didn't seem right. I had trouble sleeping last night, thinking of you locked up in that barn."

Somehow that put an end to the conversation. We finished the rest of our breakfast in silence, and moments later were back on the road. It was a long way yet to Paris—at least another two hours of hard riding.

Fifty miles or so before Paris, we stopped at a gas station to fill up. The gas attendant gave me a long, hard look, but I paid in cash and he didn't ask any uncomfortable questions.

Pierre showed me the flyer about the pickle contest. We examined it together as the motorcycle's tank was being filled.

"*Deadline for submission of your jar: precisely twelve noon on the day of the contest,*" I read.

"There's probably a train from Paris to Bern at three o'clock today," said Pierre. "The same one I was *supposed* to be on yesterday."

"What's the time now?" I asked the gas attendant, ignoring Pierre's insinuation.

"A quarter past eleven," he replied sourly.

"That leaves barely more than twenty-four hours until the contest," I said to Pierre. "But that's not really a problem. That three o'clock train will get to Bern by the evening. It's a cinch." Pierre nodded. Something told me it wouldn't be that easy.

It was one o'clock when we reached Paris. And a good thing too—it was a tough drive—even for me, the Great Aurore. The long, lonely highway abruptly turned into a wide city street with all kinds of people, shops, cafés, buildings, and monuments. It was suddenly very loud.

"Where to now?" shouted Pierre over the din, as we drove down rue Lecourbe with the rest of the daytime traffic.

"The Lyon train station, of course," I said. "We can still catch the three o'clock to Bern."

"We?" asked Pierre.

"*Oui*," I replied.

CHAPTER 6

Paris Is Perilous

You probably know that "oui" means yes. Oui? Oh, I'm not sure why I decided to go with Pierre to the pickle contest. Perhaps I was just curious if he would win. Perhaps I couldn't resist a cross-country adventure. But I think it was something else. There was a mystery before me, and I wanted to get to the bottom of it. What was the mystery? Are you not beginning to guess? I'll give you a clue—it has something to do with Pierre . . .

It should have taken half an hour for us to cross Paris—a right down the busy street rue Lecourbe, a left on pretty boulevard St. Michel, and then over the dark Seine river. Then we should have reached the Lyon train station, where our speed train would be departing for Bern, Switzerland.

And being a sophisticated and cultured girl who had certainly seen her share of Paris, I did not feel it necessary to dawdle at any of Paris's extraordinary landmarks. Pierre, of course, was dead set on reaching the train on time, and we could have been passing through a Peruvian swamp and he would not have noticed the difference. Yet still, there is a tender spot in my heart for one Paris landmark, and that is naturally *la Tour Eiffel*—the Eiffel Tower. Something about its sharp, meteoric rise to the top appeals to me, for some odd reason. And so, as we rode down rue Lecourbe, I slowed the motorcycle for a moment, and came to a stop, to take in the Eiffel Tower in all its splendor.

"What are you waiting for, let's go!" said Pierre impatiently.

I'm not one who likes to be rushed, so I stubbornly continued to gaze at the top of the tower, remote and silent as it was, above the din of Paris. It was then that I perceived that the perfect, pointy top of the tower was not so perfect and pointy as I had remembered it. In fact, there seemed to be a kind of ugly black glob protruding from the very tip—a shape that expanded somewhat as I was looking at it. Pierre, now exasperated, followed my gaze, and was also staring at this strange shape.

"What's that black thing on top of the tower?" asked Pierre with a tinge of anxiety in his voice.

I didn't answer. As we looked, the black glob detached itself from the tower and began to glide through the air, like a great dark vulture, its wings spread wide. Mesmerized, we stared at it, as it arced through the air, high over Paris, and then swooped down, down, in more or less our direction.

"I'm not sure we should wait and find out," I said finally. Pierre nodded in agreement. I revved up the engine and began to drive, faster this time, down the boulevard and away from the thing.

Pierre turned his head to look behind and up. "It's getting closer!" he said. I sped up, weaving in and out of cars and buses. When we hit a red light, I turned to look. And then I saw her clearly: a lithe woman in black tights, a mask covering most of her face, swooping down, directly toward us, with hungry vulture wings, or more correctly, a vast black hang glider.

"Duck!" cried Pierre. I did more than duck. At the last second, just as she stretched out her clutches to grab at Pierre, I threw myself to one side, causing the whole motorcycle to fall to the ground. The dark shape grasped, missed Pierre by a whisker, and passed over us, empty-handed. "Awwwww!" we heard her birdlike voice cry.

"La Renardette," I whispered.

And so I should explain that while my grandfather's henchmen were not exactly what I would call "civilized" or "cultured," there was one of his associates who was of a different caliber. He met her a long time ago and enticed her to his brood of scoundrels after an unpleasant incident that had to do with a circus and a tightrope that had been "accidentally" cut. She had a name, but that name was long ago forgotten. I heard of her seldom, but when I did, it was with the following appellation: La Renardette. A *renard* is a fox, a *renarde* is a vixen, and a *renardette* is—well, I suppose something even more cunning and devious.

Who was La Renardette? She was a shadow. She could enter a room without being detected, and leave it with all of the inhabitants' possessions, without them having noticed a thing. She was darkness. At night she thrived; in the day she was a rumor. She had the ability to melt into her surroundings like a chameleon, and to perform acts of vile deception like a serpent. She was my grandfather's most trusted confidante, and yet he did not trust her. That was well—I'm not even sure she trusted herself.

That's why when my grandfather discovered that I had rescued Pierre from his power, I have no doubt he merely brushed it off as a minor battle— he had not given up on the war. Instead, he called in his secret weapon.

"Let's get out of here!" said Pierre. We pulled ourselves up, jumped on the bike, and ran the red light, not waiting to see if La Renardette would make another dive.

"I know a shortcut," I said. I didn't really know a shortcut, but it seemed like the right thing to say at the moment. "Good," said Pierre. I made a sharp left, down a narrow alley, heading roughly north and east toward the Seine river. I knew that we should be taking one of its many bridges if we were to make it to the train station on the other side.

At the end of the alley, we took a right toward the Seine. All the while, Pierre kept stealing furtive glances back to see if we were being followed.

Within minutes we were on boulevard St. Michel, heading up over the Seine river on a long bridge. Here the river was at its widest, and we were now in a row of speeding cars with a nasty drop into deep water on both sides.

Just as we approached the center of the bridge, I saw it. The black birdlike shape was swooping down at us from directly ahead. In a second or two, La Renardette would be upon us!

There was no way I could throw down the motorcycle here in the middle of traffic—we would be run over by the speeding vehicles behind us. There was absolutely nothing I could do.

But Pierre did the strangest thing. He released his hold on my waist, and to my utter surprise, he got up on his feet and stood, perfectly balanced, on the seat of the moving bike.

"Are you crazy? Get down!" I shouted, looking back at him.

La Renardette reached out her talons once more, and a sly grin (which I could see clearly) appeared on her features as she prepared to grab Pierre. But Pierre calmly raised his left arm and pointed a single finger in front of him, holding it exactly straight ahead, unwavering. In an instant, his finger and La Renardette's nose would collide.

A startled look of confusion came over La Renardette. Pierre's arm passed between her outstretched talons. The moment of impact came. *Thunk!* I felt the motorcycle shudder, braced myself for a fall, but was shocked to find that we had not fallen over. Then I was even more shocked to find that Pierre was still onboard. Somehow, with a lone finger, Pierre had knocked La Renardette off her balance and saved us. "What happened?" I gasped. I looked back, just in time to see the black batlike figure of La Renardette twist off erratically and plunge into the depths of the Seine river. *Splash!*

Pierre sat back down quietly. I continued to drive, shaken.

"What happened back there?" I repeated, breathless. "How did you get rid of her?"

Pierre lowered his head and looked away. "I'm not sure," he said quietly.

We were safe for the time being—but we had a train to catch. And we had to find a parking spot for my motorcycle—there was no way to take that on a train, I'm afraid. After stopping some bystanders (and drawing some stares), we were told of a long-term underground lot near the train station.

"We'd better hurry up," said Pierre, "or we'll miss the train."

"Nonsense," said I. "We've at least three-quarters of an hour before it leaves."

We were about to drive down into the parking lot when I caught a glimpse of two young children trying to cross the traffic-congested rue de Rivoli. They looked nervously at the passing cars and trucks. Now, I may have been on an adventure with a time limit, but when the Great Aurore sees children who need help, she is the first to come running. After all, mine is the purest of hearts.

"What are you doing?" exclaimed Pierre as I

stopped the motorcycle on the side, got off, and walked toward the children. They had backpacks on and were obviously coming back from grade school.

"Come back!" called Pierre as I took the children's hands and carefully crossed the street. They each gave me such a wonderful smile when we got to the other side. Oh, how I love little children.

"What?" I said to Pierre, getting back on the motorcycle. "Can't one perform a little act of kindness here and there?"

"Those children would have been fine," said Pierre. "It's us I'm worried about."

"No, you're just worried about yourself and your precious jar of pickles," I said. "You think I'm selfish? You're the selfish one."

Before our argument had a chance to develop any further, we heard a loud honk. I turned around. It was my grandfather's black Cadillac! My grandfather smiled at me from the driver's seat and gave a short wave as his two henchmen got out from the side doors. Our little delay had been costly.

"Borsht!" cried Pierre. "Let's get out of here!"

I needed no encouragement. I floored the gas,

but directly in front of me was a large Metro bus. The only way to go was down into the parking lot. Without thinking I swerved away from our pursuers and zoomed down into the lot.

"Stop!" cried the lot attendant, frantically pushing a button on his console.

"Watch out!" I shouted to Pierre as the white barrier arm came down upon us.

We both bent low and the motorcycle sped under the barrier, which barely missed us.

My grandfather's helpers were not so lucky. They both ran headfirst into the barrier and were thrown to the floor, cursing.

With twists and turns, I navigated the narrow parking lanes, spiraling ever downward. A minute later we were on the bottom level: six.

Pierre and I got off the motorcycle and made sure we had our bags.

"Good-bye, *ma chérie*," I said to my poor new motorcycle, stooping and kissing it on the headlight. "I will come back for you soon." (As it turned out, I only got it back a few months later, with an astronomic parking bill.)

"You are unreal!" said Pierre, grabbing my hand. "Let's get out of here!"

We ran together down the row of cars and toward the stairwell.

We hadn't gone up four steps when we heard voices coming from above.

"I think they got to the bottom level," said a heavy, rough voice.

"Then what are we waiting for? Let's get them!" said a lean, thin voice.

We turned around to head back into the lot, but just then Pierre pointed. In front of us was the bright glow of headlights from my grandfather's Cadillac. We were trapped!

Pierre, evidently panicking, looked around frantically, clutching his jar of pickles tightly. I, of course, am cool as a cornichon in desperate situations such as these.

Well, perhaps I was screaming just a little.

Suddenly Pierre yanked my hand and pulled me down and around the bottom stairwell. Underneath the angle of the stairs was a small door, no higher than my waist.

A sign on the door read ENTRY FOR WORKERS ONLY.

"Quick!" cried Pierre as he opened the door and led me inside, into a low, shadowy passageway.

I closed the door behind us, and it was completely dark.

"Where do you think we arrrrrrrr . . . ?"

My question was cut short, as we both found ourselves tumbling down a narrow set of stairs into the darkness.

"Are you okay?" asked Pierre.

"A little bruised," I replied as we picked ourselves up at the bottom of the stairs. "Did the pickles make it?"

"Yes," said Pierre. "They're all right."

We appeared to be in some sort of tunnel. There was a dim light somewhere ahead, and the ceiling was higher than before. We could hear a *drip-drip* sound, like the sound you hear in stalactite caves. The air was dank and cool.

"We must be in some underground passageway," I said. "I wonder . . ."

"It won't be long before they figure out where we are," said Pierre. "Let's go."

We held hands and began to make our way down the tunnel toward the light. There didn't seem to be any other option.

At the end of the tunnel was a burning torch, hung on a wall, beside a wide doorway. The door was made of old thick planks of wood, and it had a heavy bar across it. The bar appeared to be locked shut.

Above the doorway there was a sign:

CATACOMBES EST—ENTRÉE INTERDITE (EAST CATACOMBS—ENTRANCE FORBIDDEN)

Pierre and I looked at each other.

"Aren't the catacombs where they used to bury the dead in the old days?" said Pierre.

I nodded.

"Well, anyhow, it's bound to be locked," said Pierre, pushing the bolt. The door swung open with a loud creak.

I smiled.

"I'm not going into an ancient cemetery that says ENTRANCE FORBIDDEN," said Pierre.

"Why not—are you scared of ghosts?"

"Yes," said Pierre. "Aren't you?"

The brave Aurore is not scared of petty human spirits (my apologies to any who are reading these lines).

"Let's go," I said, taking the torch from the wall.

"I knew you were going to say that," said Pierre, following me.

The catacombs were filled with numerous

twisting passages, not unlike a labyrinth. After several twists and turns, we could hardly remember where we had come from.

Soon, on the side of the main passage, we began to pass several low doorways that I assumed contained ancient crypts.

"Care to visit any old relatives?" I asked Pierre as we paused beside one of these. Inside, we could see a long rectangular box of stone that looked like a coffin. Pierre shuddered and shook his head.

After a few more lefts and rights, a certain fact became obvious to us.

"We're lost," said Pierre.

"Well, at least we're safe," I said.

"*Ooooooooooooo—ooooooooooo . . .*"

"Was that your stomach, Pierre?" I asked hopefully.

Pierre looked at his stomach. "I don't think so."

"*Ooooooooooooooo—oooooooooooooooooo . . .*"

The sound was getting closer. We looked ahead. A dark shadow loomed up from just behind the next bend. The shadow grew—it was coming closer.

"Run!" I shrieked calmly and without panicking whatsoever.

We turned and ran this way and that—after a

few turns, we could have been running in circles. The *ooooooo—oooooo*'s were getting louder and seemed to be coming from all directions at once. Suddenly, we found ourselves running straight into a large room with a long coffin in the middle. On the side of the room were eerie green and blue lights. And the sound of *ooooooo—ooooooooo* was echoing through the entire chamber.

"It's a ghost!" said Pierre, pointing ahead.

I looked at the ghost. She was swaying on a kind of stage, singing a sorrowful love song. She was wearing heavy lipstick and a glittering dress.

"*Ooooooo—ooooooooo, l'amour perdu . . . ooooooo—perdu, perdu . . .* (Ohhh, lost love, it's lost, it's lost)," she wailed into the mike. Our "ghost" was an aspiring lounge singer.

In a flash, it became clear to me that we were not in an ancient crypt, but in a very modern (if slightly hard to find) nightclub.

Pierre and I breathed a sigh of relief. We looked over the club. To the right, there was a bar—the source of the colored lights. The table in the center of a room, which we had thought was a coffin, was actually a billiards table. Several men got up from the bar and walked over to us.

"Good," I said to Pierre. "Perhaps these gentlemen can show us the way out of here."

The men were dressed mostly in black undershirts, they had large tattoos on their bare arms, and each had a long black beard.

"Tie them up," said the largest and tallest of the men. One of the others came and reached toward me.

Darn! Just when one begins to have faith in society, somebody comes to ruin it for you. I decided that it was time to put my jujitsu skills to good use. After all, what's the point of learning martial arts if you never use them?

"Hi-yah!" I jumped onto the table, lunged through the air, and threw a flying butterfly kick at the man. I caught him square in the stomach. He gave an *oof!* and fell to the floor, gasping. Then I ducked under another man, came up from behind him, and delivered a deadly chop to the back of his leg. He collapsed in agony. Finally, I jumped up six feet in the air and swung both feet toward the leader, crushing his nose and leaving him disabled and crying for mercy . . .

CHAPTER 7

Duel in the Catacombs

Well, at least that was the plan. I think I only got as far as the flying-through-the-air part. After that, I must have been caught. Besides, have you ever seen a twelve-year-old girl take on a band of full-grown criminals before?

"You're a real ninja," said Pierre sarcastically.

"Hey, at least I put up a fight," I retorted.

We were tied up back-to-back, and had been propped up on the billiards table. Some of the men were fingering our bags, and would soon no doubt find the jar of pickles. The head bandit walked up to us, planted his feet, and crossed his arms over his chest.

"I'm François," he said, "and no one trespasses the *Tigre Vert* without my permission," he said.

"Is that the name of your pet?" I said petulantly. *Tigre Vert* means "Green Tiger."

"No, mademoiselle," said François, "It's the name of this club—*my* club. Now, it just so happens that a friend of mine called me and said that two good-for-nothing children might be lurking around my place—I suppose he was referring to you."

"Your club isn't very hospitable if this is how you treat your guests," I said. "Perhaps we should try out that other secret underground nightclub we were looking for, eh, Pierre?"

Pierre ignored my little joke. "What do you want with us?" he asked François.

"I was wondering if your girlfriend did all the fighting *and* the talking," he answered. "Her bark's almost as good as her bite." Here François rubbed some teeth marks on his arm, which coincidentally matched my upper canines.

"She's not my girlfriend," said Pierre.

Good! I thought. At least he's got that straight.

"Hey, boss," said one of the other criminals, "look what we found here—a jar of cornichons!"

"Wonderful," said François, turning to us. "It's just after lunchtime and my men are hungry for dessert. Crack it open, Perrault."

"Don't open that!" cried Pierre, squirming against the cords.

"Oh ho!" said François. "Looks like we found something valuable. What's so precious about the pickles to you, boy?"

"I'm taking them to a contest," said Pierre, before I could stop him.

François grinned. "A contest, eh? Well, perhaps we can let you know our personal opinion. Perrault, hand me that jar."

Perrault handed François the jar. Pierre was becoming frantic. If they opened the jar, the pickles would lose their freshness, and we wouldn't have a chance of winning the contest. *Don't do it, don't open it!* he prayed.

François was about to open the jar when his eyes became very wide.

"*Cornichons La Bouche,*" he read slowly. He looked up at Pierre. "Who's La Bouche?"

"I am," said Pierre.

"Are you—are you related to *Jo Jo* La Bouche?" asked François with a sudden quiver in his voice.

Oh no, not this again.

"Yes," said Pierre, smiling a little. "He's my younger brother."

"Untie these children," said François immediately. "And don't touch their bags."

François's men reluctantly put down our bags and began to untie us. When it was done, François gingerly handed Pierre the jar of pickles.

"Okay," I blurted out. "This is too much. I can't take it. What in the world has Pierre's little brother got to do with anything? Why does the name La Bouche keep getting us out of jams?"

François sunk down on a nearby chair and sighed. "Jo Jo La Bouche saved my daughter's life."

This has got to be good, I thought to myself.

François continued. "Last year, I took Manon— that's my little girl—to the annual Paris parade. I had just turned my back to get her an ice cream, and before I knew it, she had grabbed a handful of those floating balloons from one of the stands. My sweet girl is as light as a feather, and when I turned back to her, she was already out of my reach, floating up, up into the air over the parade. I was going out of my wits. Then, suddenly, this little boy takes out the straw from his soda, and starts blowing toothpicks up at the balloons. He shoots them one by one, until she comes floating down slowly into my arms. He had saved her life! 'What's your name?' I ask. 'Jo Jo,' he says. 'Jo Jo what?' 'Jo Jo La Bouche,' chirps the little hero. 'I will always remember you,' I said, and then my little Manon throws her arms around him and gives him a kiss on the cheek. She's a real beauty. This little La Bouche turns red as a strawberry and runs off into the crowd. I never got to thank him properly. But now . . ."

That's when my grandfather and his two henchmen marched into the club.

My grandfather was wearing his favorite trench coat and had on his sunglasses, as usual.

"Ah, François," he said, approaching us. "I see you've found the little scoundrels. You've done well. But why are they untied? Never mind, I'll take this from here. Aurore, you've strayed quite far from home, and it's about time I brought you back. Pierre, hand me that jar of pickles—now!" My grandfather reached out toward Pierre.

"Hold on a moment," said François, pulling my grandfather's arm back. "I can't let you take that."

All of a sudden François's henchmen were snarling face-to-face with my grandfather's cronies. Both sides smelled a fight.

"Is this how you treat an old friend, François?" said my grandfather menacingly.

"I'm sorry, Zacharie," said François firmly, "but I owe a debt to this boy's family. I cannot let you take them."

My grandfather sized up the situation. François's men outnumbered his, and he was not on his home turf.

"I see," he said, more politely. "In that case I suggest an alternative to force. Here before us is a billiards table. I say that the jar of pickles belongs to me. The boy says it is his. Why don't we settle this like gentlemen?" As he said this, he lifted two cues off the wall, handing one of them to Pierre. "If you win—you keep the jar. If I win—the jar is mine."

François seemed to be pleased with this compromise. "That sounds fair," he said. His men began to back down.

"What?" I said. "You expect a mere boy to beat

an old shark at a game of pool?" Everyone looked at me as if I were mad. "Pierre," I said, turning to him, "have you ever played billiards in your life?"

"No," said Pierre.

"Well, then, that's it. We're going." I took Pierre's hand, and started to walk toward the exit. We were stopped by my grandfather's men, who blocked the way. I looked pleadingly at François.

"I'm sorry, *ma chérie*," he said apologetically. "I'm afraid this is the best I can do for you."

Pierre and I slowly turned back toward the table. "I've *seen* people play pool before," Pierre said, gulping.

"Perhaps this game will teach you not to meddle with powers above your head," said my grandfather, sneering.

One of François's men set up the balls on the table. When the solid-colored and striped balls were in place in a triangle, he reached out to place the white ball, the cue ball, in position.

"That won't be necessary, lad," said my grandfather. "I prefer to use my own."

At this, my grandfather removed his sunglasses, and then, to Pierre's dismay and my disgust, he plucked his glass eye out of its socket and placed it on the table instead of the cue ball. Later, looking back at that eye trick, I realized that if my grandfather wasn't purely evil, then at least he was seriously twisted.

"Care to begin?" he said to Pierre.

"No, you go first," said Pierre.

My grandfather chuckled. I closed my eyes. This was going to be too hard to watch.

My grandfather took the break shot like a seasoned expert, and I could tell by the reaction from his men that some of the balls already went into the pockets. "I'll take stripes," he said to Pierre, "and you're solids."

A few more shots, and a few more balls had gone down. I knew it. My grandfather took pride in these "gentlemanly" parlor games of precision, and I was sure he would win after another minute or two.

"Blast!" he exclaimed. I opened my eyes in time to see him miss. "Your turn, boy."

Pierre got ready to make his first shot. *How am I going to get out of this one?* he wondered. He nervously grasped the cue stick, like someone who'd never picked up a cue in his life. And to make things worse, he had been just average at everything he tried—tests, races, feats of strength. He never came in first place at anything. He knew he had no chance whatsoever. Leaning over awkwardly, he attempted to make the shot.

This whole thing is an absurd joke, I thought. I shut my eyes tightly, this time.

"What?" I heard my grandfather exclaim. I opened my eyes just a bit. I was in time to see Pierre's second shot. I watched in disbelief as the cue ball (my grandfather's eye) knocked sweetly into two solid balls, sending them both into the holes in perfect symmetry. Pierre had begun to smile.

By the third shot, François, his men, and my grandfather's men were all eagerly watching Pierre.

"*Zut alors!*" cried François as Pierre's next shot hit its mark, and sent yet another solid ball down the hole.

I looked at my grandfather, who was grinding his teeth.

"Pretty shots, boy," he said, "but you're through now. This next shot is impossible—even for a master."

It was true. We all looked at the table and

saw that the last two solid balls were completely blocked by a clump of striped balls in the middle of the table.

Pierre furrowed his brow and bent down low, sliding the cue back and forth on his hand. "Come on, come on," he murmured.

He can't make this shot, he can't make this shot, I thought to myself.

Plunk! Pierre's cue hit my grandfather's eye at its base. The eye popped into the air, sailed over the striped balls, and landed with a *bang!* back on the table. Still moving fast, it crashed into the two solid balls that were left and knocked them both into the corner pockets.

"Yes!" cried Pierre. The room was speechless.

"The back left pocket," said Pierre as he took a shot at the black 8 ball, and easily knocked it into the pocket he had named.

Pierre had won the game!

François and his men whooped for joy and slapped Pierre so hard on the back that he nearly fell over. "Another one for La Bouche!" cried François, unable to hide his pleasure.

"How—did—you—do—that?" I whispered to Pierre in awe.

Suddenly Pierre became uncomfortable. He shuffled his feet and would not meet my gaze. "I don't know," he said.

"Well, Zacharie," said François, turning to my grandfather. "The boy has beaten you fair and square, eh?"

My grandfather had turned a queer shade of purple, and I thought he would burst. Instead he took a deep breath and sighed. Picking up his eye and putting it back into its socket, he turned to Pierre.

"Indeed, Pierre. It seems that I have somewhat underestimated you. The pickle jar is yours." Then he looked at his wristwatch and gave us an evil grin. "But I'm afraid you may have missed your train . . ."

At that, he glared at me, put on his sunglasses, and stormed out of the room with his men.

I looked at my watch and then at Pierre.

"He's right," I said mournfully. "The train leaves in five minutes . . ."

CHAPTER 8

A Fox Trap

I should have realized I had just witnessed a miracle. How could my Pierre, who had never played a game of pool before, beat a master like my grandfather? Yes, my simple Pierre, a boy who had never won anything in his life—a cornichon. The whole thing was impossible. But as we were shuffled up François's secret staircase by his men, as we raced across the alley to make a mad dash for the train station, parts of the puzzle were beginning to fit into place for me.

Of course, I hadn't too many clues to go on. Really, there were only two: Pierre's shocking victory at pool, and our desperate encounter with La Renardette over the Seine river. And as we sped past the crowds of people and straight to the ticket booth, a third thought occurred to me as well— how had Pierre not fallen off my motorcycle in those first few seconds, when he was holding on to nothing at all (besides a pickle jar), and I was recklessly swerving down that bumpy country road?

"Two tickets to Bern!" I said to the ticket master, breathlessly.

"You're too late," said the woman. "The train is leaving now."

We looked past the ticket gate and into the station. I could see the last passengers boarding the speed train. Any second and the doors would close.

"Please!" I said. "It's a matter of life and death!" (Okay, a little exaggeration, but hardly a lie.)

"I'm sorry," she said, "but you'll have to wait until tomorrow. There's nothing I can do."

A wild impulse occurred to me. "This boy's name is La Bouche!" I said, pointing at Pierre.

"So what?" said the woman, already turning to the next customer.

Well, it was worth a try.

The whistle sounded, and the doors of the train closed. We watched with wide eyes as it pulled out of the station without us, carrying our hopes of winning the contest with it.

"You *had* to stop for those two children," said Pierre, turning to me.

"What?" I said. "What are you talking about?"

"I mean, you had to help those two children cross the street," he repeated. "If you hadn't done that, Borsht wouldn't have seen us, and we'd be on that train to Bern."

I narrowed my eyes. I couldn't believe what I was hearing. "You're blaming me? But those children might have been hit by a car. At least I have a big enough heart to help others."

"If you have such a big heart," said Pierre icily, "why did you kidnap me in the first place?"

"Oh, so that's what this is all about. Well, you know something, Mr. Pickle Belly, I'm not so sure I should have saved you at all. You don't deserve—"

"Did I overhear the name La Bouche?" said a twangy voice with a Texas accent, interrupting our pleasant exchange.

We turned. A tall, broad-shouldered man in a

green soldier's uniform was standing before us. He had an army beret on his head and was wearing goggles around his neck.

"As a matter of fact, yes," I said pertly. "This is Pierre La Bouche. And I suppose his second cousin twice removed saved your village from a famine."

"Not exactly," said the man. "The name's Klinger, Captain John Klinger of the U.S. Army 23rd Paratroopers Division. Are you by any chance related to a fella named Henri La Bouche?" he said, looking at Pierre.

"Henri La Bouche is my grandfather," said Pierre proudly.

I'm having *déjà vu*, I said to myself, shaking my head.

"Well, I'll be darned," said the man. "I'm standing here today because of your grandfather."

I had had quite enough of these outrageous coincidences. "Look, sir," I said, "I'm afraid that we're in a terrible rush. You see, we need to get to Bern by tomorrow noon, and we've missed our train. So if you'll excuse us, we'll be leaving now."

"Oh, okay," said the man. "I'm sorry to be a nuisance. Of course, my men and I are planning a landing near Geneva this afternoon. We're doing a little joint parachuting exercise with the French and Swiss armies. And if Henri La Bouche's grandson would be interested," he said, tipping his beret toward Pierre, "it would be my honor to have him along for the ride—and his lady friend, if she'd be obliged."

"I am not anybody's *lady friend*," I said in a huff. I reached down to pick up our bags.

"Thank you, Captain Klinger," said Pierre. "We'd be happy to join you."

I turned to Pierre and gave him a searing look.

"What is it, Aurore?" he asked.

"Pierre," I began, "if you think I'm about to get into a strange plane, and fly up to who knows where—"

"Are you scared of heights?" Pierre interrupted.

The Great Aurore is not afraid of anything, let alone being high above the ground, in a dizzying aircraft, not knowing if and how I was going to land. Well, perhaps I was just a little bit uncomfortable about heights—but I don't think "fear" is the appropriate word.

"Are you okay?" said Captain Klinger, looking at me. "You just got a little green around the gills."

"Fine, fine," I said. "Hah, I'm not afraid of

heights—when do we die? I mean, when do we dive?"

"Oh, *you* won't be diving," said Klinger. "We'll leave the parachuting to me and my men. But the pilot can land you anywhere you like near Geneva."

That already sounded somewhat more reasonable. "I see," I said. "Well, then, when do we take off?"

Half an hour later, we found ourselves at a small military air base just north of Paris. Klinger had been waiting in the train station to pick up some of his men. He had driven us all to the base in a green army truck, and now that his crew was assembled, we were almost ready to take off. Several engineers were servicing the plane, and Klinger was briefing his men on the training exercise.

"Are you going to be okay?" Pierre whispered to me, with a hint of concern.

"Me? What, who, me? Of course I'll be okay." I suppose I had been breathing just a little bit faster than usual. "It's you I'm worried about," I said. "You look a little pale—are you sure you're ready to get into that flimsy thing?" I said, pointing to the small olive-colored airplane before us. It really did look quite flimsy.

Pierre looked at me and shook his head. "Hey, it's okay to admit you're afraid of something, Aurore," he said. "It's perfectly normal."

Before I could deliver an appropriately zinging reply, Klinger came over and handed us two flight suits and a pair of earphones.

"These are for you to wear," he said. "When we get up to a higher altitude for the jump, you'll need the earphones to maintain your ear pressure and be able to communicate."

Pierre and I put on the flight suits and walked over to the plane with Klinger.

"All aboard," called Klinger, and we got in. It really was quite a small aircraft, and the ten of us had to squeeze in so that we could fit, what with all the extra equipment Klinger's men were taking. Did I say ten? Well, there were really eleven, but the eleventh wasn't seen or counted by any of us at the time.

"How do you know my grandfather?" Pierre asked Captain Klinger, as the plane rose to 15,000 feet.

"You might as well ask how I *don't* know your grandfather," said Klinger. "My papi—that's my dad—wouldn't stop talking about him. Ya see, son, back in World War II, my papi was in one of those units that landed in Normandy to fight the Germans. Your grandfather was in a French resistance unit back then. His unit and my papi's fought in the same battles.

"Now, one day, when the fightin' was worst, my papi's unit and your grandpapi's found themselves in the same gosh-darn trench. They were about twenty men there, stuck between a hail of German crossfire. To make things worse, the whole trench was filled with about fifteen barrels of dynamite, and if anything lit that pile on fire, the whole twenty would have been blown sky-high. Now, suddenly, out of nowhere, this flare lands in the middle of the trench. I ain't got no clue how it got there, but at that second it was the most dangerous thing that could have shown up—and it was lit. What does good ol' Henri do? He takes that flare and he stuffs the lit end in his mouth—just as it starts to go off. My papi said his whole face and cheeks lit up like a Roman candle—but he wouldn't open his mouth! Two minutes later he spits it out and the whole trench cheers. My papi swears it was Henri that saved all of their lives. And from then on, everyone called him *La Bouche*—the mouth. It became like his official name."

"That must be why Grandfather's mouth always seems so full of . . ."

"Of what?" asked Captain Klinger.

Pierre was about to say marbles, and I hardly think that would have been nice. Instead he surprised me and said:

". . . of wisdom."

"I don't know about wisdom, young'un," said Klinger, "but his heart's sure full of bravery. That man is a real hero, and I'm proud to have his grandson in my plane."

Pierre and I looked at each other, smiling. The whole story seemed so fantastical.

"And speaking of the plane," said Klinger, "you two interested in how we fly this darn thing?"

"Ah—I think I'll take a pass—," I started to say.

"Sure, we'd love to," said Pierre.

Before I could protest, Klinger took our hands

and led us into the cockpit. There sat his pilot at the controls—a youngish soldier named Jackson.

We looked out the front window. Ahead, it was all blue sky and clouds. Below, far below, was French farmland, so far away that it looked like a remote patchwork of greens and browns.

Klinger began pointing out the controls to us.

"This is the control yoke—that's like the wheel of a car . . . here's the throttle—that's like the gas pedal . . . here's the rudder control—you'll need that to land the plane (not that you'll be landing it yourselves) . . . and here's where you put out the landing gear . . ." I was mainly trying not to look down. Pierre seemed more interested.

"Can I give it a try?" he asked.

"Sure, I don't see why not," said Klinger. "Here, have a seat. Jackson—let this boy take the joystick for a bit, how 'bout?"

Pierre was still holding the jar of pickles (he never let it down if he could help it). He must have been so keen on flying the plane that for some strange reason, instead of handing the jar to me, he put it down on the floor of the cockpit.

Pierre settled into the pilot's seat and grasped the

controls. The plane sailed effortlessly through the air.

"Why, you're a real natural," said Klinger. "This boy'll be a pilot someday."

At that very moment, two dark, shady hands slipped into the cockpit. They closed around the jar of pickles. A second later, the hands were gone, and a jar of pickles remained.

Pierre was so pleased with his flying that for the next few minutes, he was totally preoccupied with it. Even after Klinger said, "All right, boy, I think you've had enough for now," and we'd gone back into the cabin with the other men, I think Pierre was still up in the clouds, pretending he was at the controls. There was something about flying a plane that spoke to him. And I suppose that's why neither of us thought to pick up the jar of pickles from the floor of the cockpit.

Klinger came back to the cabin with us to get his men ready for the jump. Jackson, the pilot, was left alone in the cockpit. As it turned out, he had missed breakfast and lunch that day, and was "mighty hungry," as he muttered to himself. He looked around for something to nibble on. His eyes lit on the jar of pickles not two feet away from him. "Golly," he must have said to himself. "Well I'll be darned. This is just the thing to tide me over."

"Okay, men, it's about time we blew this popsicle stand," said Klinger to his soldiers. All of them got their parachutes ready.

"Hey, the pickles!" said Pierre suddenly. He ran back into the cockpit, scooped up the jar, and came back into the cabin.

Klinger slid open the wide door on the side of the plane. It was suddenly very loud and windy in the cabin. We put on our earphones. Klinger's men began jumping out of the plane with their parachutes. Pierre watched as they floated down toward Earth, like little dots. As I am not overly fond of gazing down at sickening 20,000-foot drops, I conveniently found something important to adjust on my flight suit.

"Well, I guess this is it," said Klinger to us. The last of his men was getting ready to jump. "It's been a real sweet pleasure gettin' to know you folks," he said. We shook his hand, and he pumped ours up and down. At that exact moment, another passenger—not one of Klinger's paratroopers—

got ready to jump. Perhaps it was her first time, and maybe that's why she hesitated for a second. Klinger turned around.

"Hey, you're not one of my men!" he exclaimed. The imposter didn't give him much time to digest this information. Her head was covered by a dark hood, but her red lips formed a smirking smile. "Seee you laterr, litttlle peeeople," she hissed at us (it sounded like a snake speaking). With that, she jumped out of the plane, clutching a jar of pickles. Klinger dove after her. "You get back heeeeeere!" we heard him shout, as the wind and air swallowed up his last words.

Pierre and I scrambled to the edge to see what would happen.

Klinger and the woman were struggling over the jar, each pulling at it with all their might as they plummeted down through the atmosphere. The last thing we saw was the jar of pickles popping out of both their hands, and tumbling down, down, down toward the Alps without a parachute.

I struggled to digest what I had just seen. Who was this woman who was dressed up as one of Klinger's men and had jumped out of the plane with the jar of pickles? The realization hit me like a cold splash of ice water. "La Renardette!" I whispered. "I should have known."

It came to me in a flash. Not all of the engineers had left the plane when we boarded it. One of them wore engineers' clothing, looked and acted like an engineer, but was not an engineer. And as we soared over the rolling mountains and ice blue lakes, she hatched her plan.

"Who was that?" shouted Pierre. "Was that the same lady we met over the Seine?"

"Never mind," I said. There would be time to explain later. The main thing right now was the pickles. I looked at Pierre. He was holding the jar of pickles he'd taken from the cockpit.

"Are those your pickles?" I shouted.

We surveyed the jar. The familiar CORNICHONS LA BOUCHE was written across the front. It certainly looked like our pickles. Before we had time to look any closer, the plane suddenly lurched to the left, and down. We were thrown to the floor.

"What's going on?" I shouted. Pierre and I, on our hands and knees, crawled across the floor and into the cockpit. There, a disturbing sight greeted us. It was Jackson, on the floor of the cockpit, breathing heavily, his eyes closed. His face had an awful greenish hue.

"Wake him up!" I shouted.

Pierre shook Jackson, even slapped him across the face. But the poor pilot was out cold. The plane lurched left again, and we tumbled across the cockpit floor.

"We're gonna die!" I screamed.

Pierre looked up at me. "No," he said, "we're gonna fly."

He scrambled into the pilot's seat and grabbed the controls.

The plane plummeted through the air, heading toward white-capped mountains below.

I could see the meters on the dashboard turning around wildly and took that as a sign that all was not well.

Pierre struggled with the control yoke and set his teeth. "If I can just get ahold of it," he whispered. The plane stopped veering to the left and righted itself. But we were still heading down, down, at a terrifying speed.

All I could do was not to panic completely. I looked ahead. We were already not far from the ground. Did I say ground?—well, not exactly.

The Alps are a high and majestic range of mountains that run from France and all the way through Switzerland, Italy, and Austria. And we were going to get to know them a little too closely.

"Over there!" I shouted, pointing. In front of us, looming larger and larger each second, were two enormous mountains, side by side.

"I see them," said Pierre.

"Try to get between them," I said. That seemed to be our only hope. Certainly, crashing into one or the other was not a good idea.

Pierre pulled the plane to the left, and for a second, it seemed we might turn over completely. Then he corrected himself, and we were heading toward the small space between the mountains. It was going to be close.

Faster than I could have ever imagined, there were two giant walls of snow and ice approaching us from both sides. A small crack between them was all the space left. "Almost there," said Pierre tensely, "almost there." At the last second, he jerked the controls to the right, and *skid!* We were through, the left wing of the plane scraping across the wall of ice and snow.

"Whew," I breathed. "Nice flying."

"Now for the landing," said Pierre, wiping the sweat off his brow. I gulped.

They say that landing a plane is actually safer and easier than taking off. That might be true—if you have a runway.

"Over there," said Pierre, pointing toward a relatively flat-looking plateau of snow or ice ahead of us. Slowly, and with what I later understood to be utter balance and precision, Pierre lowered the plane down toward the "landing field." Soon, the plane was hovering just a few feet above the snow, and a moment later, we were bumping across it.

"Easy, easy," I said. "Wait—the landing gear!"

It was too late. The plane was already skidding across the snow and ice.

"Hold on!" cried Pierre, and he gave one last push on the control yoke. The plane twisted and turned this way and that, and suddenly it flipped half over and thudded to a terrific stop, shooting up mounds of snow into the air.

"Everybody okay?" asked Pierre.

"Yes, if you'd get your shoe out of my face," I said.

"Sorry," apologized Pierre, picking up his foot.

"Nice landing."

"Thanks," said Pierre. "I couldn't have done it without you."

Well, I'm not sure how true that was, but at least it was a nice thing for him to say.

I kicked the door of the cockpit open. It took us about ten minutes to lug Jackson, the semiconscious pilot, out of the plane and onto the snow. We pulled our bags out of the plane, and Pierre made sure he had his pickle jar.

"Well, we're alive," I said. "But where are we?"

We surveyed the terrain. Behind us were the two mountains through which we had flown. Ahead was a series of lower hills that eventually faded into what looked like trees and small lakes. Far, far away, what looked to be a village peeped out in the distance. It could have been twenty miles or a hundred—it was difficult to tell.

Pierre was staring at the jar of pickles. He wouldn't take his eyes off it, except to look back and forth to the pilot every few seconds.

"What is it, Pierre?" I said.

"There's something not right," said Pierre. "That woman—the pilot—this jar. There's something not right."

We bent over the pilot to see how he was faring. He was breathing a little easier, and seemed to be mumbling something.

"Ohhhh, never shoulda, never shoulda... never shoulda tasted 'em ... worst tastin' things I've ever hadddd . . ." He drifted into incoherent muttering, and then was silent. He seemed to be in a fitful sleep.

"Maybe we should try one of the pickles," I said.

"We can't do that," said Pierre. "If we open the jar, the pickles won't stay fresh."

The Great Aurore knows when she's right. Before Pierre could think, I snatched the jar out of his hands, and began running with it over the snow. Pierre was close on my heels, but as I said, he's only an average runner, and I run like the wind. I had soon outdistanced him. I knelt down and opened the jar. Pierre didn't tackle me—he was scared to knock over the jar. He just stood there and scowled. I produced a pickle and put it to my mouth. I took a tiny bite—and chewed.

It was like chewing on a dead worm covered in moldy slime.

"Eeeeeeeewwwww!" I shrieked. "This is groo-oooosssssssss!"

I spit out the revolting excuse for a pickle onto the snow.

Pierre was flabbergasted. I handed him the jar. "Here, you try," I said.

Pierre slowly took the jar and extracted another pickle. "They look like my grandfather's pickles," he said. He sniffed it. "They smell like my grandfather's pickles."

He put it in his mouth. And closed it.

Then he began to chew.

That's when he spat out the whole thing directly in my face.

"Oops, sorry," he said. "Yup—definitely not my grandfather's."

I had pieces of the disgusting pickle in my hair and all over my face.

"Why, you!" I picked up a clump of snow and threw it at Pierre. It got him square in the neck.

"Hey!" said Pierre, dropping the jar and scooping up some of the white stuff. Soon we were having a full-blown snowball fight.

Pierre may be a good pilot, but he's just a mediocre snowball fighter. Within a minute I had him pinned to the floor and spitting out mouthfuls of snow that I'd stuffed in his face.

"Okay, okay, stop!" he cried.

"That'll teach you some manners," I said, getting up. Well, it had also been fun, I have to admit.

We sat down on the snow and assessed our situation. I explained to Pierre about La Renardette and how she had obviously stolen his jar of pickles and switched it with another, inferior jar.

"So my pickles are somewhere in the mountains," he said, as the situation came home to him. "These are fakes, and we're stuck here in the middle of nowhere."

"Yes," I said, "I think you've got it."

"Well, we might as well have crashed the plane," said Pierre. "I can't win the contest now." He slouched down onto the snow, beaten.

"Hey," I said, bending down, "that's no way to talk. We'll find some way out of this mess."

"You don't understand," said Pierre. "If I've lost the pickles, there's no point anymore. I've failed."

I had an impulse to say something incredibly witty, but instead, a lump caught in my throat and I blurted out, "No, Pierre. You haven't failed."

Pierre swallowed. He watched me for a second without saying anything.

Suddenly, I had an idea.

"You can make your own pickles," I said.

Pierre looked at me like I was nuts.

"That's it!" I repeated, *"You can make your own pickles!"*

Pierre shook his head. "I don't know the first thing about making pickles, Aurore. My grandfather was in charge of the whole thing. He let my mom and dad help out—even Chantal and Jo Jo had jobs. But I was never really good at anything, so they never let me get close. I can't do it. I don't even have a clue where to start."

"You didn't have a clue how to play pool or how to fly a plane, and look—you did great. Why can't you do the same thing with pickles?"

"I don't know how I did those things, Aurore," said Pierre. "Maybe it was just luck. To make pickles you need more than luck—you need skill. And I've never been skilled at anything. I'm a cornichon, and that's that."

"That's no excuse not to try," I said.

"In any case," said Pierre, ignoring my logic, "pickles take time to ferment. There's no way they could be ready by tomorrow. They need at least two weeks. Pickles! Here we are talking about making pickles while we're stuck here in the middle of nowhere. How are we going to get out of this place?"

Just then, the sound of barking could be heard. We swiveled around. I was just in time to see Pierre knocked over by a very large dog.

It was a Saint Bernard, and it was licking Pierre's face.

CHAPTER 9

Mountain Magic

You are probably beginning to guess what Pierre's special talent is. The motorcycle chase, the pool game, and now, the "miraculous" plane landing. If you're still in the dark, then I won't give away his secret quite yet. Unfortunately, in this chapter something happens that will throw me off the trail, so to speak, for some time. But I assure you that when the Great Aurore gets her hands on a mystery, she doesn't let go until she gets her man.

The giant, shaggy Saint Bernard, or Fluffy, as we had begun to call him, was of great service. After he tackled Pierre and ascertained his well-being, he proceeded to examine the unconscious pilot. He managed to elicit a low moan from Jackson by licking his face and neck all over, covering him with a layer of foamy Saint Bernard saliva (which has well-known therapeutic properties). I noticed a small bottle around the beast's neck, just like in the movies. I unscrewed the cap, and poured a few drops of the dark, syrupy liquid into Jackson's mouth. Jackson moaned again, but this time, his pouting lips curved into a smile and his cheeks became rosy. Seeing this, Fluffy gave us a series of short, eager barks, and took a few leaps away from the plane, which we clearly understood was his way of saying "*Après moi*—Follow me."

We got our gear together and, using a blanket from the plane, created a sort of makeshift stretcher or hammock for Jackson. Fluffy was overjoyed to be strapped to this device, and together the four of us began to trudge across the snow in the direction of the nearest slope.

The way was not easy. At some points, the snow

was as deep as our knees, and the temperature was close to freezing. After a while, our path snaked downward, and I understood that we were making our slow way down the side of the great mountain. Eventually, the snow got less deep, but the wind began to pick up, and it bit our uncovered faces mercilessly.

After about an hour of this, just when I thought I couldn't go any farther (and I don't need to tell you that I have incredible endurance and willpower—I certainly wasn't complaining out loud—or out too loud), Fluffy began barking again and jumping up and down in the air.

"Look," said Pierre, pointing at the ridge. Before us, on the ridge's right-hand side, stood a beautiful-looking log cabin. Whether it was the trick of the landscape or some force of nature we couldn't perceive, the cabin itself was completely free of snow. Surrounding it on three sides was a marvelous greenhouse. Yes, a greenhouse, right up there among the Swiss Alps. As we made our way to the entrance, I caught glimpses of green leafy plants and vegetables within its sunbaked walls. As we approached the gate, I surveyed the landscape below the house. It seemed that just a few hundred yards down, there were grassy slopes, while a few hundred paces above the house was a blanket of snow and ice. Clearly, this house was on the exact border between the everlasting winter of the mountain and nature's changing seasons below.

"*Bienvenue*—Welcome!" called a clear, light voice. We looked up. There, coming down the wooden stairs, was a girl who looked to be not much older than us, with bright carrot-colored hair and emerald green eyes. She had a gracious, pleasant face, but when she smiled, I thought I saw a vague mischievous look. "I see Frédéric has found you lost in the wild. You are very welcome here. My name is Rochelle." She came down to greet us and we trudged up to her. "Look," she said, "you have an injured man. I will do what I can to help him."

Together with Frédéric (we weren't far off calling him Fluffy), we managed to carry Jackson up the steps and into the mountain lodge, where we had set him down on a bed in one of the rooms. He was still moaning, so Rochelle brought him a mug filled with some steaming, odorous liquid. The half-conscious pilot took one sip of this, let his head fall back onto the pillow, and immediately fell into a deep, contented sleep.

"I am sure he'll be fine," said Rochelle. "I'll now attend to some of his things. You may wait for me in the living room."

While Rochelle went to hang up Jackson's wet clothing, we checked out her living room—even I was impressed by it. The furniture was all hand-made out of carved wood; there were beautiful, rich paintings on each wall, delicate sculptures on the mantelpiece, and several exotic-looking plants dotting the floor. I have an eye for good taste, and this living room had it!

"I'm sorry," said Rochelle, entering the room, "for not letting you introduce yourselves. What are your names?"

"I'm Aurore," I said, taking her hand. She had a firm grip. I'm no slouch either, so I squeezed as hard as I could, but the funny thing was, when she let go, it was my hand that stung.

"Pierre," said Pierre, shaking Rochelle's hand as well. When they shook hands, I noticed that Rochelle looked hard at Pierre, going over his face with her eyes for a long time. That put me off a little. Pierre, for his part, turned his eyes away from hers, and I believe I noticed him blush!

"Where are your parents?" I asked Rochelle,

trying to move things away from awkward intro-
ductions.

"I'm afraid to say that my parents are no longer
with me . . . ," said Rochelle.

Here she became embarrassed, but I could not
resist probing just a little. "You mean you live here
alone?"

"Well, with Frédéric, of course," said Rochelle.

Again she was looking at Pierre. Now Pierre
was eyeing her curiously too. Well, I had had quite
enough of this!

"I see," I said. "That must be quite a challenge. In
any case, thank you for helping us with the pilot.
But you see we're in a terrible rush—we must be on
our way now. Pierre?"

Pierre seemed to be preoccupied with a painting on the wall. "I've seen that painting before . . . ,"
he said slowly. It was a painting of a boy in
bed, being tucked in by his mother. The mother
had red hair. *Where have I seen that?* thought Pierre.
And then—*home!*

"Oh, yes, it's a beautiful painting," said Rochelle,
ignoring me. "It's one of my favorites. Ah, won't you
stay for dinner? It's almost ready and I rarely have
guests up here in the mountains."

"Thank you very much," said Pierre before I could intervene. "We would be happy to stay."

"Wonderful," said Rochelle. "Dinner will be ready in ten minutes."

When she went off to the kitchen to finish preparing the meal, I grabbed Pierre by the elbow and dragged him to a quiet corner.

"Why should we stay here with this—this stranger?" I whispered to him.

Pierre gave me a look. "I don't see why we shouldn't stay. Anyhow, we're stranded, and maybe she can help us."

"How do you know we can trust her?" I said.

"I'm not sure," said Pierre. "It's just—it's just that I get a very familiar feeling about her, as if . . ."

"As if what?"

"As if I've known her for a long time," said Pierre with a dreamy, far-off look.

"Dinner is served," announced Rochelle as she brought in a platter of food from the kitchen.

I put on my best plastic smile, which is only half as dazzling as my real smile, and prepared to have a perfectly rotten time.

"So what brings you here this far up in the mountains?" asked Rochelle, looking directly at Pierre.

We were eagerly wolfing down what I had to admit was the freshest and most delicious raclette and green salad I had consumed in a long time.

"We're touring Switzerland by foot," I said quickly, before Pierre could respond.

"We're doing nothing of the sort," said Pierre. "We were trying to get to the world pickle competition in Bern, before we lost our pickles and our plane crashed."

I gave Pierre a swift kick under the table, which made him spit out his mouthful. He shot me a sharp glance.

"A pickle competition!" said Rochelle. "That's wonderful. I *love* pickles. Actually, I've been making them myself for decades—I mean years." She wiped her mouth with a napkin.

I certainly didn't miss that slip-up. What did she mean, "decades"? I looked up at Rochelle's eyes with curiosity. Her face, her figure, her hair—they all looked like that of a thirteen- or fourteen-year-old. But there was something different about her eyes that I couldn't put my finger on . . .

"How old are you, Rochelle?" I said sweetly.

Rochelle coughed, pretending not to hear my question. "Oh, I almost forgot—the tea!" She quickly got up and whisked off into the kitchen, only to appear five minutes later with herbal tea and dessert—peaches and cream.

"You know," she said to Pierre, "I am growing cornichon cucumbers in my greenhouse. Most of them are ripe for the picking. If you like, after dinner, we can pick some and make pickles right here in my kitchen."

Pierre thought about it for a second. "Okay," he said slowly. Then he turned to me with a polite smile. "Aurore was just saying how I should try to make my own pickles. Weren't you, Aurore?" I gave him another kick.

I flashed Rochelle a wide, toothy, plastic-wrapped grin. "We'd be delighted," I said, giving Pierre one last kick for good measure. Pierre stifled a yelp.

Rochelle's greenhouse garden really was something special—even I had to admit that. There were plants, shrubs, trees, fruits, and vegetables of every kind, shape, and color, all growing happily under the sun, in a land that was completely out of place for them. We loaded up Frédéric with baskets of cornichon cucumbers, onions, garlic, and dill. All the while, Rochelle prattled on incessantly about her experiences up in the mountains (which was the only annoying thing about the tour—she had such an old-fashioned way of speaking—it reminded me of my great-aunt, may she rest in peace).

"And that's when the Germans tried to invade Switzerland from over the pass. It was close to the end of the war. But the Swiss army and our French allies sent sharpshooters to line the upper ridge and prepare for an attack. Some of them stayed in this cabin. They had such deep voices and sang wonderful songs of the mountains. Later they took out their alphorns and played into the night—it was beautiful—I mean, I mean, from what I've read," she finished quickly.

"What are those herbs over there?" Pierre asked curiously, pointing to a set of deep purple shoots on a nearby table. A sign underneath the pots read LA JEUNESSE ÉTERNELLE.

"Oh, those?" Rochelle said, with a quick turn of her head. "Those are nothing special. Just a kind of mountain weed—I collect them for fun, but they're not of much use."

In my head, all sorts of alarm bells were ringing. *Jeunesse Éternelle* literally means "everlasting youth." How could something with that name be "nothing special"? I just couldn't swallow what I was hearing for the plain truth.

Back in the kitchen, we laid out the ingredients for the pickles. Rochelle had assembled an array of airtight jars, which Pierre and I had helped sterilize by boiling, and we were now ready for the bottling process.

"Wait!" said Pierre. "There's something I want to do." Pierre reached into his pocket and removed a blue envelope—the same one his mother had given him at the beginning of his journey.

"What's that?" I asked.

Pierre didn't answer right away. He appeared to be lost in thought. He slowly opened the envelope and gazed at the letter. "It's a recipe . . . ," he murmured.

Soon we were selecting the best cornichon cucumbers from the batch—only the ones with the little nubs on them—and putting them into the jars. A cornichon cucumber is much smaller than an American cucumber, so you can fit a whole lot into one jar. We cut up pieces of garlic and cloves and put some in, as well. It was almost time for the vinegar and brine solution.

"Hold on," said Pierre. "Aurore, could you pass me that dill?"

"Oh, Pierre," said Rochelle, "that's not for the pickles—I just brought it in for tomorrow's salad. Dill is what Americans use in pickles, isn't it?"

"That's right," said Pierre, "and we're going to use it in these. Look."

Pierre showed us the recipe. It was his mother's gift to him before she waved good-bye. The title read: BROOKLYN PICKLES—THE BEST IN THE WORLD. The final ingredient was indeed dill. It was signed "Myron Polotnik." Pierre's mother had written a line below that.

My dear Pierre, this is my father's recipe. You never knew him—but maybe by using it, you'll find out what kind of man he was. I'm sure he would be proud of you. I know I am. Love, Mom.

"That's a beautiful note," said Rochelle.

"An American cornichon," I said. "It'll never work."

Pierre held up the dill. "We'll see," he said. And he thought, *This is it—this is how to make them the tastiest.*

In the end, since he was so stubborn, I gave in, and let him stuff a good amount of dill into one of the jars.

"Now for the brine," said Pierre, rubbing his hands.

Pierre carefully poured the pickling salt into the pot of water. Rochelle was about to add half a bottle of vinegar when Pierre said, "Hold on—that's too much. Allow me."

Gingerly, he took the bottle and poured in some vinegar. He dipped his finger in the solution and tasted, then poured in a little bit more.

"Perfect!" he declared when he was done. Rochelle and I both watched in fascination.

We brought the brine to a simmer. Then we poured it from the pot into the jars. Finally, we sealed the jars, carried them to the pantry (which was not far away from the kitchen door), and placed them on a windowsill. Cucumbers become pickles through a funny chemical process called "fermentation," and putting them in sunlight speeds the whole thing up. Rochelle remained in the kitchen to clean the dishes.

I stayed in the pantry a moment longer to stack up some empty jars. When I quietly walked back to the kitchen, I saw the following scene:

Rochelle was humming an old wisp of a song— it sounded like a lullaby.

She began to sing softly:

Little baby, my sweet baby,
You are resting in my arms,
The day is gone,
The night has come,
And now it's time to sleep,
While the stars shining bright,
Are dancing overhead . . .

Pierre, standing close by, finished the last line:

. . . it is you, dearest boy, I will tuck into bed.

Then he walked over to Rochelle, and they stood face-to-face.

"It's a beautiful lullaby," she said. "But how did you know it?"

"You know how I know it," said Pierre. "That was the lullaby my father sang to me . . ."

As he said this, Rochelle reached up and put her hand on his cheek.

I had seen enough. I guess I didn't know what I was doing—I turned around, got my things, and without thinking I burst through the front door and down the steps. My eyes were red, and I suppose I was crying. I hardly noticed, but I still had one of the pickle jars in my hands—the same one that Pierre had prepared. Had I stayed outside the kitchen for one more moment, I would have heard Pierre finish his sentence:

". . . Grandmother."

CHAPTER 10
Cliff Hanger

I don't remember how long I walked in snow, across fields of ice, up and down slopes, but always downward, downward. Perhaps I'd had enough of this absurd adventure. Maybe I just needed to be in my own bed, on my own farm, at home. Who was this Pierre, anyhow, who troubled me so much? What did I care if he met some other girl in the mountains, and I never saw him again? Who was he to make me cry? I did not have the answers to these questions.

Eventually, even my extraordinary endurance ran out. Night was falling, and soon the golden stars were really dancing overhead. In my own head, a very different kind of dance was taking place. Yes, I admit it—this adventure was starting to get the better of me, and I felt like I couldn't understand what was happening to me, let alone go onward.

I kept on walking for what seemed an eternity. A cold wind blew down from the mountain. I felt my cheeks—they were frozen. *I must find a place to rest*, an instinct in me said. I kept on walking.

Finally, perhaps five minutes later or perhaps five hours, I saw before me something that looked like a long giant snake in my path. *A tunnel over the ground?* my mind asked. It was, in fact, completely blocking my path. I looked this way—it continued; I looked that way—it continued. It was quite tall—perhaps two stories high, so I couldn't imagine scaling it—certainly not in my condition. I walked up to it, felt its sides—it was made of sleek black metal. "What on earth is this thing?" I murmured. I was so tired that I didn't really care. I slumped against it and tried to lie in the crack between it and the ground.

The temperature was dropping. *You can't survive the night like this,* I thought. I forced myself to get up. I began walking, I know not why, along this strange overground tunnel, not having a clue what I would find. After a few minutes, I did find something. It was what looked to be a doorway. Where the handle or doorknob would have been, there was a metal wheel, like the kind you'd see on ships or submarines.

"It's sure to be locked," I said. A biting wind tore at my face and cheeks. In desperation, I put down the jar of pickles, grabbed hold of the wheel, and yanked down on one side with all my might. The wheel began to turn! I kept on turning it until I heard a whine—and then a click. The heavy metal door opened. Without thinking, I picked up the jar of pickles and climbed inside the tunnel, shutting the door behind me.

Inside the tunnel, it was at least much warmer. The walls were slick white and that was all. No decor, no floor, no ceiling—just a pure white tube. I did not care. I lay down on the floor of the tube, with the jar of pickles on my chest, and fell asleep.

Some of the things you have read about in this book so far have been perhaps just a tad hard to swallow. When you read them, were you asking yourself: Could that really happen? When Aurore said that everything in the story was true, was she twisting the facts just a little? Can Aurore really be trusted? Well, I'll have you know that first of all, after everything we (you and I) have been through, I'm just a little bit hurt that you would suspect me in that way. I would hope that by now you would be completely on my side, ready to eat out of my hand if I asked it. No matter. I care not what others think of me. Well, then, okay, I admit it—what you are about to read is, even for me, a tiny bit difficult to accept, and I forgive you your doubts if you have them. But I say this: believe it or not, *it happened,* and that's what's important.

Pierre was sitting opposite Rochelle at her kitchen table. The room was silent. The air was tense, as if it were electrically charged. Rochelle found that she could not speak. Her aged eyes were now cast down, so that to the observer she looked like an ordinary fourteen-year-old.

"What happened to you? Why didn't you tell me?" asked Pierre, looking at his grandmother directly.

"I—I wanted to tell you, Pierre," said Rochelle. "Seeing you make pickles just now brought back so many memories. It so reminded me of—of . . ."

"Of Grandfather, right?" asked Pierre.

"Yes," said Rochelle. "Of my dear Henri. I started to sing the song we used to put your father to bed with, when he was just a young boy. I hoped you would recognize it, and by it, recognize me. I've been so alone all these years." Rochelle's voice cracked, and a lone tear descended from her cheek.

Pierre persisted. "But why did you leave Grandfather in the first place? He never speaks about you. Whenever I asked him about you, he always changed the subject—as if—as if he wanted to forget you."

"Pierre," said Rochelle slowly, "this may be hard for you to understand. I loved your grandfather very much, but we had so many differences. He was one of those soldiers that came to defend this land from the Germans. I fell in love with his deep voice and the beautiful music he made. We were married in the spring. At first, it was wonderful. We would live together in the mountains and make our life together. But then, he spoke more and more about the farm of his father in France, and of his dream of rebuilding it. But I didn't want that. I wanted to be free on these beautiful hills and live forever. He told me that eternal life is nothing if you never fulfill your dream. In the end, even though it was he who left me, it was I who drove him away, to follow his dream. And now I see that he has, and I am happy for him."

Pierre stared ahead at his grandmother. Suddenly he recalled the family meeting, remembered how his grandfather had turned red at the suggestion that he himself go to the contest. *"Who knows?* She *might be there,"* he heard his grandfather murmur. That was it! *She* was Rochelle, Henri's wife! That was the real reason he didn't want to go. He was afraid she might show up at the contest, and then he would have to face his past . . .

But there was still some terrible mystery here. "How are you young, Grandmother?" asked Pierre. "You speak about eternal life. What have you done to yourself to get it?"

Rochelle got up from her chair and held out her hand. "Follow me, Pierre," she said. "I can only show you, and you will decide if to believe."

Together, they once again entered the greenhouse. Rochelle brought Pierre to the row of purple herbs that were labeled La Jeunesse Éternelle.

"Your grandfather and I found this herb one morning in our young days as we wandered on these slopes. We found a bird, a very old bird. It was dying. I had—I had an instinct. I fed the bird this herb. And by the next morning, it had flown away—young again."

"You mean this herb makes old things young?" asked Pierre, full of wonderment.

Rochelle skirted the question. "Pierre, your grandfather refused eternal youth. I did not. Would you refuse to remain young forever? Would you stay here with me, and live free, always a happy boy, never to grow old and die?" Rochelle held out her hand in a gesture of welcome.

How can I refuse my own grandmother? thought Pierre. He looked from the purple sprigs to his grandmother's hand. Should he take it? Lost in indecision, he turned away and cast his gaze ahead over the slopes, into the distance. "There's something I'm forgetting," he murmured. "Something missing . . ."

Then he saw it. My footprints leading out of the

gate and toward the slopes beyond. "Aurore," he murmured, and then shouting loudly, "Aurore!" He dashed off, running around the house, and then inside it, desperately searching for me, calling my name. A minute later, breathless, he stood once again before his grandmother.

"She is gone," he said, hanging his head.

"I know," said Rochelle. "But won't you stay?"

Pierre shook his head. "I love you, Grandmother, and I would stay here with you. But I must save my friend. She trusted me, and I have failed her."

Rochelle looked beaten, lost, but after a moment a tiny smile emerged on her lips. "I understand, Pierre. You too have a dream, and you must follow it. I am so proud of you. Go, and save your friend!"

Pierre surged forward and hugged his grandmother. She held him tight for a moment, and then released him. "Go, Pierre. Go before it is too late." Pierre turned to leave.

"Wait," he said, turning. "Why don't you come with me? Why don't you return with me to Grandfather?"

"No," said Rochelle, shaking her head. "I'm afraid it is too late for that, Pierre. Someday you will understand." Pierre nodded. It was true—he did not understand.

A moment later, Pierre had gathered his things and was prepared to leave. Rochelle promised that she would take care of Jackson until he had fully recovered.

"Take Frédéric with you," she said. "It's the only way you'll catch up. And take some of these," she said, picking a few sprigs of La Jeunesse Éternelle. "You never know when you might need them." Rochelle whistled loudly, and Frédéric bounded over. Pierre mounted him and allowed Rochelle to press the purple sprigs into his hand. He placed them carefully inside his shirt pocket.

"Won't you be cold?" asked Rochelle. Grandmothers, after all, are grandmothers.

Pierre smiled and kissed his grandmother goodbye. He turned once and waved, as he and Frédéric galloped off after my footprints. "Good-bye, Grandmother, good-bye!" he called. Rochelle waved goodbye and turned back toward her home.

Pierre rode over the snow at great speed on the back of the giant dog. That must have been a brilliant run—over a white field, under the sparkling night sky. He almost cried out loud from the joy of it. I'd like to think it was also the joy of running after me.

And what of me? Well, as I lay in a deep sleep, on the immaculate white floor of that long tunnel with the pickles on my chest, something began to happen. Had you been there, you would have seen tiny streaks of blinding light shooting down that tunnel, passing us, going over us, going through us. The jar bubbled. Inside it, changes were going on. The firm, green cucumbers began to take on a different hue, to twist and to shrink. And my skin was beginning to wrinkle . . .

Snowflakes began to fall. Pierre brushed them away from his eyes and concentrated on my footprints. "We've got to go faster, Frédéric," he said, "or the snow will cover her tracks." Frédéric seemed to understand. He picked up his trot to a gallop, and soon he and Pierre were flying across the snow in a blur, hot on my trail.

The flakes made the ground soft and powdery.

Frédéric barked gladly as he ran, and Pierre too opened his mouth in delight. Then, without warning, Frédéric's front paws hit a patch of ice, which had been thinly veiled by the new snow. "Sttoooopppp!" cried Pierre. But it was too late. Already he and Frédéric were sliding wildly away from the trail and off to the left, toward—Pierre gasped—toward a bare cliff face, and beyond it, a gaping chasm!

Pierre fought to stay on top of the Saint Bernard as Frédéric struggled to regain his footing. In moments, they were a few paces away from the brink. At the last second, just as Pierre thought the end had come, he saw a single gray stone jutting out from the snow. Without stopping to think, he lunged for it—and caught it!

Now he was hanging from the stone, grasping it with both hands, as his feet dangled over the nothingness below.

"Frédéric!" Pierre shouted, looking down into the chasm.

To Pierre's surprise and relief, the giant dog had

caught onto his foot and was hanging from it by the mouth. "Owww!" cried Pierre as he felt himself being stretched.

Slowly, steadily, Pierre was being pulled downward. And try as he might, his slippery, freezing hands were losing grip on the stone. "Hang in there, Frédéric," he called to the dog, but without much hope.

Pierre was becoming delirious. He gazed up at the stone he was holding. It was rounded on top, and strangely, it seemed to him that it looked greenish in color. *Like a pickle*, thought Pierre. The pull on his legs was becoming unbearable.

"Why don't you just let go?" said a voice inside his head.

"I can't!" shouted Pierre into the wind.

"Is it me you want so badly?" said the voice. Pierre looked up, and now it seemed to him that he was holding on to a giant pickle, and that the pickle was talking to him. *I must be dreaming . . .* , he thought.

"Am *I* all you care about?" said the voice.

"This is crazy," Pierre whispered. But he thought about it. Was it true? Was winning the pickle contest all he cared about?

"No," he said. "There's Aurore . . ." As he said this, Pierre gritted his teeth and clutched desperately at the stone. It had become a regular stone once more. Pierre looked down. Then he saw it. A few feet below, a smaller ledge jutted out, not far from Frédéric. Using his last strength, Pierre began to swing his body like a pendulum, back and forth. Frédéric was getting closer and closer to the ledge.

"Jump, Frédéric!" called Pierre. The dog, as if he understood, released his hold on Pierre's feet and made a lunge for it. Somehow, using all four paws, he managed to claw his way up the ledge to safety.

Pierre felt he could hold on no longer. "Go, Frédéric, go!" he called to the dog.

But Frédéric, not willing to give up, reached down with his shaggy head and caught Pierre by the shoulder, tugging up hard. There was a breathless moment of struggle, and then with a lurch, the two of them were lying side by side on top of the cliff, panting.

A moment later and they were up.

Frédéric began to bark eagerly, sniffing the snow

and pointing his nose southward. He had clearly picked up a trace of my trail.

I almost died just now, thought Pierre.

He looked west, toward Rochelle's house. He could still go back there if he wished, and give up the quest.

But then Pierre raised his face toward the heavens. There, high overhead, were the glittering stars. One of them, the morning star, sparkled brightly near the horizon. "Aurore," he said for the third time that night, "we're coming for you."

Pierre gave Frédéric a pat on the head. "Come on, Frédéric, we're going to find her," he said. With that, he jumped onto the Saint Bernard's back, and was off in a flash of white, back on the trail.

Soon, the two of them were standing in front of the enormous tunnel.

"She can't have gone in there," said Pierre to Frédéric, who was barking and sniffing at the door of the tunnel. Pierre looked down at my footprints, which ended right at the door, in dismay. Even Pierre, who is no great detective, could come to no other conclusion.

He grasped the wheel and began to turn it. Soon he had opened the door and looked inside. A strange sight met his eyes. There on the floor lay an old, wrinkled woman, clutching a jar of completely fermented and ready-to-eat pickles. Pierre blinked. The old woman was wearing my clothes. She opened her eyes and looked into Pierre's. He recognized her. Or to be more precise—he recognized me.

That's right. The old woman *was* me! Somehow, in that strange white tunnel, I, beautiful, breathtaking Aurore, a girl in the prime and flower of her youth, had been cruelly transformed into a tired and wizened old lady who could barely lift her head to meet Pierre's horrified gaze.

I can forgive Pierre for screaming. "What happened to you?" he gasped. I tried to get up. It was difficult. All of my bones and joints creaked and cracked.

"I don't know," I said to him. "Why are you looking at me like that? What's happened to me? Why can't I move properly?" I said in a weak, gravelly voice.

We gazed at the jar of pickles. They appeared to be completely done and ready.

"You're—you're old!" said Pierre bluntly. He never had too much extra tact, but I'll forgive him for the moment.

I reached up and passed my hand over my face. I felt my cracked, wrinkled skin. The truth was beginning to dawn on me.

"This tunnel, this tube—it makes things age," I said slowly, without much strength. "Look at it—me, the pickles. It's some kind of magic . . ."

"It's not magic," said Pierre. "I don't know what it is. But we've got to get you out of here."

Looking back, I can't believe I didn't panic—I, glamorous, resplendent Aurore, discovering that I had suddenly become old and withered. But I suppose that was just it—my mind too had been withered and numbed into submission.

"I can barely move," I said. "You go on. I'm too old. I'll die soon. Take the pickles, go win the contest. Do it without me."

Pierre looked at me in shock. "Don't say that, Aurore." That made me smile a little.

"Thanks for coming to rescue me," I said. "Even though it's too late."

Pierre pretended not to hear that. With all his strength, he dragged me out of the tunnel and into the open air. I could hear Frédéric barking and yelping around me. I looked up. It was almost day-break. The wind had died down. I felt as if I were going to die down as well.

Above the wind, or beyond it, I could hear a fluttering sound. It sounded like a large bird. I did not care anymore.

"Good-bye, Pierre," I said, closing my eyes.

Pierre shook me, "Don't go, Aurore!" he called desperately. *"Not after everything we've been through,"* he whispered. His voice was fading away.

The fluttering sound became louder, and we were now bathed in the eerie glow of a helicopter's rescue lights overhead. My head fell to its side.

"Wait!" cried Pierre. He pulled something out of his jacket pocket, crushed it up in his hands, and put in into my mouth. Just as I lost consciousness, I was aware of a sweet taste in my mouth, sweeter than anything I had ever tasted in my life. I supposed it was the taste of heaven . . .

CHAPTER 11

Accelerated Stuff

I opened my eyes. I was in a white room. I raised my head. I appeared to be wearing a new set of white clothing and lying on a soft, white surface. *If this is heaven*, I thought, *then at least it's nice and clean.* I felt my skin, my face—it was smooth. That was a relief. I didn't feel like spending my afterlife as a wrinkled prune. The door to the room opened. A very short, squat woman wearing a white gown walked over to me. She wore incredibly thick glasses, and her hair was pulled back into an extremely tight knot.

"Good," she said. "I see you are awake." Then

she produced a small, metallic instrument that looked oddly like a stethoscope, and pointed it at me. A bright green light shot out from it and passed over my head and my body. I squinted. After a few seconds, she turned off the light and looked at the device closely.

"Amazing," said the woman. "You are perfectly restored. There are no molecular imbalances, hardly any cell damage."

"Where am I?" I asked, getting up on one elbow.

The woman raised an eyebrow. "Have you ever heard of CERN?"

The name rang a bell, but a very faint one that seemed quite far off. I stared at her blankly.

She let out a brief sigh, as if to bemoan the lack of knowledge of today's youth. "CERN is the *Conseil Européen pour la Recherche Nucléaire*—European Council for Nuclear Research. These days, we say 'Organization,' not 'Council,' but never mind that. What matters is that it is a scientific laboratory shared by the nations of the world to investigate nuclear particles—the tiny building blocks of our universe."

"So we're in CERN?" I asked, trying to act like I followed her.

"Heavens no," she said. "We are in DERN, which is very much like CERN, except that it is absolutely secret and very few people in the world know of its existence. And now that *you* are one of them, allow me to introduce myself. I am Dr. Esti Muon, the director and founder of DERN. And you are lucky to be alive."

I shook Dr. Muon's hand. She had a viselike grip, which was especially remarkable for somebody her size. "What does the 'D' in DERN stand for?" I asked.

"Don't ask," said Dr. Muon icily.

"Darn," I said.

"DERN," she corrected.

I looked around. "Where is Pierre?" I said, suddenly remembering him.

Just then, the door to the room opened and Pierre walked in. He came up to my bed and smiled at me, and I could see that he was both surprised and relieved to see me young again.

"How did you save me?" I asked him.

"It was my grandmother's herb," he said quietly.

"Your grandmother?" I asked.

"I'll tell you about it another time," he whispered.

Dr. Muon came forward to us. "You children are not aware of it, but this girl and her jar of pickles have gone through the first biological particle acceleration experiment ever."

"Sure, *I* understand that, Dr.," I said, getting up and putting on my best scientific expression, "but maybe you should explain it to Pierre."

"Of course—I forget that not all people are high-energy particle physicists," said Dr. Muon with a twist of a smile (I could see she was somewhat of an eccentric). "This institute conducts experiments using what appears to be just a very long tunnel. Through this tunnel we shoot extremely tiny particles, like atoms, electrons, protons, at extremely high speeds. And we see how they change, and what new particles are created. The tunnel is called a particle accelerator. And that is the tunnel that you were in when we turned the accelerator on. When the particles accelerated through your body, they aged you prematurely, just as they aged your jar of pickles. What I don't understand is how you became young again."

Pierre put his finger to his lips when she said this, but I didn't need that sign to know that his manner of rescue was to remain secret.

"Well, I see that there is some mystery here," said Dr. Muon. "That is fine with me. But with your permission, I'd like to borrow your jar of pickles for more analysis."

Pierre and I exchanged glances. "We need the pickles, Dr. Muon," I said. "We've got to bring them to a contest in Bern."

"Yes, Pierre has told me. But this will only take a few minutes," said Muon, "and I won't even have to open the jar."

"We owe you our rescue," said Pierre. "And without your accelerator, we wouldn't have these pickles. Let's do it."

"I thank you," said Muon, bowing. "Come with me."

Pierre helped me up (I was beginning to feel myself again) and we followed Dr. Muon down the hall, into an elevator, and down several floors toward what must have been a very deep basement.

"What happened to Frédéric?" I whispered to Pierre as the elevator descended.

"I sent him back to Rochelle," he whispered back.

Dr. Muon interrupted our exchange before I could ask any more questions about my rescue.

"The particle laboratory is far under the earth,

in order to avoid interference from alpha waves and cosmic radiation," she explained.

"Ohhh," I said.

"Alpha waves," repeated Pierre.

We exited the elevator onto the fifteenth floor below the surface. A large laboratory sprawled before us, with a vast quantity of machines, experiments, and scientists dressed in white lab suits. Dr. Muon led us to a station not far away and motioned us to sit down on a bench. She remained standing, beside what looked like an empty doorway. It reminded me of a metal detector I had once seen in an airport. On its left side was a large television screen.

"The pickles, please," she said to Pierre.

Pierre was reluctant.

"I see you are concerned," she said. "Do not worry, Pierre. This detector does not alter anything in the specimen. It's a phase-three atomic sensophotometer."

Well, that makes it all better, I thought.

Finally, Pierre shrugged and handed Dr. Muon the jar of pickles. She placed it on the floor, directly under the detector, and then flipped a switch on the screen.

The screen lit up, and a strange sight met our eyes. It was like a moving picture of dancing lights, swerving this way and that in a twisting flow.

"What are we seeing, Dr. Muon?" I asked.

"I'll try to explain this in a way that you'll understand," she said. "You see, everything in the world is made up of atoms. These atoms have various energy levels. There are also several types of energy they can have. What you are seeing on this screen is the energy formation of the jar of pickles. Have you ever heard of somebody's aura?"

"Now you're talking," I said, pricking up my ears. "I read all about that on the Internet. A person can have a red aura, a blue aura, a purple aura. I'm special, so I probably have a multicolored aura."

"Auras are nonsense," said Dr. Muon.

I began to protest, but she gave me a short wave of dismissal.

"Nonsense, I repeat. But the idea helps you understand what this device is measuring. What we are looking at, in layman's terms, is the pickle jar's atomic aura."

Pierre had tuned out during the last bit of the conversation and was looking at the jar of pickles. He had had enough of all the experimentation and wanted to get going to the contest. He stooped down to pick up the jar. As he did so, he hesitated for a minute, his head under the detector, watching the pickles.

"Stay where you are!" snapped Dr. Muon. I jumped. Pierre froze. "This is incredible," Dr. Muon whispered.

She bent her small face closer to the readout on the screen, and squinted at it. "I've never seen anything like this before in my life," she murmured.

"Can we move now?" I asked timidly. Dr. Muon took the jar from Pierre and motioned for him to stay under the detector.

"Look at the screen, children," she said.

We looked. The energy lines had formed a perfect sphere.

"Do you realize what this means?" said Dr. Muon. We shook our heads. "This boy's mind is in perfect energy balance. Watch."

Muon pulled Pierre away from the detector and, still holding him, went under it herself. Immediately, the energy took on a lopsided shape that looked more like a blob than anything else. "See— I'm a glob," she said.

She's right about that, I thought.

Then she pulled Pierre back under the detector, and again we saw the perfect spherical ball. It seemed to me that the ball was spinning.

"You must have an extraordinary sense of balance and precision," she said to Pierre.

Well, that began to explain a few things! The motorcycle—the pool game—the airplane landing . . . Pierre was so exactly average, his mind so perfectly balanced, that he was able to do the most extraordinary things.

Pierre was having the same thought. "What if—," he said.

"Enough!" interrupted Dr. Muon. "We have delved too deep. The experiment is over. And I have kept you long enough. Someday, Pierre, when you are ready, I invite you to return to DERN, and perhaps we can learn more about you."

"Thank you, Dr. Muon," said Pierre graciously.

"I have arranged for you to be driven to Bern," she said formally. "Your lift leaves in five minutes. Follow me."

Muon and Pierre left the laboratory station and headed toward the elevator. Out of pure curiosity, I dipped my head under the detector and looked at the screen. An erratic dance of energy met my eyes. It was like watching a hundred thousand stars at a disco, all speeding back and forth at once. No symmetry—just confusion. *Boing, boing, boing* went the lights, back and forth across the screen at a dizzying rate. Then, all of a sudden, the screen went dead and a fizzling sound could be heard. A smell of smoke arose from it.

Wow, I thought, *my mind is so wild, even the machine couldn't take it.*

"Coming," I called, running after Pierre and the doctor.

We followed Dr. Muon to the elevator and up, up, up to the ground floor.

"Here is our lobby," she said as we found ourselves in a plush, modern, tastefully decorated hall. "As you can see, it's eleven fifteen. The workers' minibus will be here any minute to take you to Bern, and you should be there in less than two hours."

"What?" said Pierre, looking at the large digital clock over the lobby. "The clock there says it's only ten fifteen. The contest closes at noon."

"Of course," said Dr. Muon, "all the clocks in this institute display Greenwich Mean Time, in England, which is one hour earlier than it is here in Switzerland. That clock," she said, pointing, as the seconds ticked by, "is the most accurate clock in the world."

"So it's one hour *later*?" I said, starting to lose my nerve. "Then we're going to miss the contest!" Pierre just stared at the clock, watching the seconds display.

"Listen," said Dr. Muon shortly. "It's been quite a busy day, and I thank you for helping with my experiments, but I really must be going." Dr. Muon turned to leave.

"*La Bouche?*" I said, clinging to a last shred of hope.

Muon turned. "What did you say?" she asked, raising an eyebrow.

"I said Pierre's last name is La Bouche—does it mean anything to you?"

Dr. Muon scuttled over to us and said in a low voice. "Are you related to Chantal La Bouche?"

"She's my sister," said Pierre, grinning. I smiled.

Muon's eyes darted this way and that. "Come

with me," she said in a whisper, grabbed our hands, and scurried toward an unlit hallway.

A minute or two later, we were standing before a black doorway. It had no knob on it, just a sort of keypad.

"The DERN institute is hidden from the world for many reasons," said Muon. "But what I'm about to show you is its deepest secret. I only ask that you keep it that way."

Pierre nodded his head obediently.

"I can keep a secret," I said, putting my hand to my heart. Pierre and Muon looked at me skeptically.

Then she placed her fingers on the keypad and the door slid open. We entered a dark room. Within it, glowing neon lights lined the floor.

In the center of the room was a circular capsule. It looked like a giant glass bubble. To its right was a console.

"Chantal La Bouche," said Dr. Muon, "helped me design the laboratory downstairs. She was on a class field trip to CERN when I met her. I saw right away that she was obsessed with cleanliness. A particle laboratory must be, as you may be aware, absolutely clean—no dirt whatsoever. And however hard one tries, dirt always enters. Chantal has a peculiar sense for dirt—she abhors it. We used her unique ability to create the cleanroom environment. I owe her my job and my reputation. And what I do now is because of that debt. Now, please, Pierre and Aurore, step into the chamber."

"What is it?" I asked. After all, someone here had to be the cautious one.

"It's a particle transport chamber," said Dr. Muon. "You go in there and come out—wherever I tell it."

"You mean—," Pierre began.

"That's right, you're going to get to the contest on time," said Muon. "There's only one thing—"

There's always one thing, I thought.

"The machine is not absolutely accurate. There is a chance—though very small—that you won't appear on the other end at the exact coordinates that I punch in."

"Well, the main thing is that we get to Bern in one piece," I said.

"Oh, yes," said Muon. "You'll get there in one piece. I wouldn't let you into the machine if that wasn't the case. It's just that appearing suddenly in the middle of some unpredictable location may not be entirely safe."

I looked at Pierre skeptically. "Let's do it," he said steadily. Fine—it was time to throw caution to the wind. We had a contest to win. I nodded.

"Okay, we're ready," I said, turning to Dr. Muon.

Muon helped us into the chamber. Inside it, there was a strange geometrical shape on the floor. "Stand in the middle of this and hold hands."

We got into place and held hands. In his other hand, Pierre held the jar of pickles.

Muon closed the chamber door and walked over to the console.

"Graubünden Hall, Bern, Switzerland," she said, and she typed in some coordinates. "Now this may feel a little weird . . ."

I can't completely describe the sensation I felt at that moment. It was like all of my limbs became spaghetti. My stomach turned into a knot, unwound itself, and then turned into an even worse knot. I was about to yell, but when I opened my mouth, it stretched and stretched and I couldn't make a sound.

For several moments everything was black, and then fuzzy objects began to come into view. A loud sound, like a waterfall, could be heard. Then, almost as if someone had switched on a lightbulb, everything suddenly came into focus. Pierre and I were standing on solid ground. We were still holding hands. There were odd-looking cement walls on three sides. Above the walls was a gate, and over the gate there were people, watching and pointing at us. Some of them had already begun to scream. And that's when I realized, to my shock, that directly in front of us, on his hind legs, was a very large and hungry-looking bear.

CHAPTER 12

The Clock Is Fast

Well, at least we're in Bern," said Pierre as he and I slowly backed away from the advancing beast. It was an understatement. The bear growled. Every French child has heard of the famous bear pits of Bern. But we never expected to end up in one of them—as lunch!

Soon we would have our backs to the wall, with nowhere to run. The bear took another few steps forward. We could almost smell his breath. Then, as things looked most bleak, I, the Great Aurore, had a brilliant idea. I snatched the jar of pickles from Pierre, twisted off the cap, and threw a pickle at the bear. The great animal opened its mouth wide and caught it. Then it chewed thoughtfully and made a noise of satisfaction. To my surprise and relief, it came up to me and nuzzled my feet. Clearly, it wanted more. I took out another pickle and fed the bear a second helping.

"Stop that!" said Pierre. At that moment we were hoisted up into the air by several hands. Two strong men, evidently in charge of the pits, had been lowered down with ropes and were lifting us up to safety. The worried onlookers were now cheering. We were soon breathing hard, standing among them.

"Those must be *some* pickles!" said one.

"You kids put on a good show," said another.

(Both were speaking in Swiss German, which I understand somewhat—my mother was from Switzerland.)

The bear keepers scolded us loudly for getting into the pit but then moved off to deal with the bear. He had evidently never eaten pickles before, and they were concerned for his well-being.

"Aurore!" said Pierre sharply, turning to me. "Why did you do that?"

"You mean why did I save our lives?" I asked.

"That bear would have eaten us if I hadn't given him the pickles."

"I had the situation under control," said Pierre, becoming hot. "But you always think you know best."

I stared at Pierre for a second with my mouth wide open. How dare he say such a thing! I'd really begun to have enough of him and his precious pickles. And can't he see that I *do* know best?

"*You* had the situation under control? How, exactly? Huh? You know what, Mr. I-have-a-balanced-brain-so-I'm-really-something-special—*you* could be a lot nicer, and more grateful. And this time—I've had it. Here! Take your pickles," I said, pushing the jar into his hands. "You can win the contest by yourself. I'm going home!" Well, perhaps a little harsh, but you really hurt my feelings, Pierre. Don't you understand that a girl has feelings?

I turned around and stormed off down the street.

"Wait!" called Pierre, running after me.

I turned around. "What is it now?"

"I'm—I'm sorry," said Pierre. "I'm sorry for being selfish, and for being rude to you. You—you saved my life, and . . ."

". . . and what?"

Pierre looked into my eyes. "And you're my best friend."

Oh, Pierre, how do you sometimes know exactly what to say?

My sour face slowly turned into a grin, and from a grin into a real, live dazzling Aurore smile—much, much better than the plastic kind. Pierre smiled back. He knew I had forgiven him.

"Enough with the mushy stuff," I said. "We've got a contest to win. What time is it?"

At that moment, we heard the gong of a clock. It was Bern's famous town hall clock. And it was about to strike noon.

Ding, dong . . .

"Quick," I said. "Where's Graubünden Hall?" we asked an onlooker. "It's not far from here," he said, pointing. "All the way down this street, and to the right."

Ding, dong . . .

I grabbed Pierre's hand and we sped down the street. The clock continued to gong.

Ding, dong . . .

We were nearly at the end of the street.

Ding, dong . . .

We turned right. There, in front of us, was the hall. People were milling about the entrance. We ran up the steps and up to the counter.

Gong! The clock had struck noon.

"Here," I said, breathless, to the man at the booth, as I set the jar down in front of him with a clang. "These pickles are for the contest."

The man didn't look up from his spectacles. "You're too late," he said, pointing to the flyer on the wall. "The contest closed at noon."

"But it is noon!" I protested. "The clock just struck noon."

"That's right," said the man quietly and without becoming ruffled in the least. "You handed in the pickles after it struck noon."

I couldn't believe what I was hearing. I mean, I had heard of being on time before, but this was outrageous.

"We're not going to just stand here and listen to this, Pierre, are we?" I said hotly.

"Your town clock is fast," said Pierre firmly.

For the first time, the man looked up. "Heh? What's that, boy?"

"I said your town clock is fast—by one and a quarter seconds."

I noticed that a little red color had entered the man's cheeks. He opened his mouth and closed it. Then opened it again.

"Our town clock," he said, sitting up straighter and raising his chin in the air, "is neither fast nor slow. It is exactly on time. It has been that way for hundreds of years."

"Then I suggest you check it," said Pierre with a hint of humor. "You wouldn't want it to be off."

"I am not about to be told what time it is by a simple boy," he said, frowning. "The rules are the rules—I can't take your jar of pickles."

At that moment, the phone in the booth rang.

The man picked it up, all the while looking at us over his spectacles.

"Yes, yes, this is Graubünden Hall."

"Two French children? Yes, they're standing right in front of me. Did they make it on time? Funny you should ask. Well, no, the contest closed at noon, and they were late. What? No, I can't accept their entry. Check my clock? Dr. Muon, I assure you— What time do I have? 12:02, of course— And how many seconds? Forty-five seconds. What do you mean, 'fast'? That's impossible. Okay, okay, have it your way. I'll check, I'll check. Thank you, Dr. Muon. Good-bye."

The flustered man got up from his seat, gave us an enigmatic look, and waddled off down the hall.

"How do you know that their clock is fast?" I said to Pierre.

"I counted," he said.

"What do you mean *you counted*?" I said incredulously.

"You remember the clock in the lobby at DERN, the one that's the most accurate in the world?"

"Yes."

"I've been counting the seconds in my head ever since we left it."

"But how can you keep track of the time so exactly?"

"I don't know, I don't know," said Pierre. "I don't know how I do these things, I just know that I'm right. Maybe it has to do with the way my mind looked on that detector—you know—balanced and everything."

My mouth hung open. The funny thing was that I believed him.

The man we had spoken to came back down the

hall. He was quite red in the face. He was huffing and puffing. But he was smiling.

"You are correct!" he said to Pierre. "We have telephoned the master clock in Greenwich. Our town clock, the pride and joy of Bern, was one and a quarter seconds fast. On behalf of this town, I thank you profusely." The man shook Pierre's hand vigorously. "But how did you know, boy?"

"Just a hunch," said Pierre, giving the man his jar of pickles.

"I will take these to the judges immediately," said the man, wiping sweat off his brow. "And I wish you the best of luck."

"*. . . because you're going to need it*," said another voice. We whirled. A tall man in a trench coat and sunglasses was standing in the entrance. It was my grandfather.

CHAPTER 13

The Winning Pickle

Pierre and I were exhausted, but we prepared to make a run for it.

"Oh, that's not necessary," said my grandfather. "You see, the race is over. I'm not chasing after you any longer. You've given in your pickles, and I've given in mine. Now we'll just have to wait and see whose are the better."

"You know, you almost got us killed up in that plane, with—with that lady friend of yours you sent after us," I said to him.

My grandfather feigned surprise. "You mean La

Renardette? Why, she's as harmless as a kitten. I can't imagine her putting you in any danger."

"She's more a fiend than a woman," I said. "Why couldn't you let Pierre get to the contest fair and square?"

"There are some things that you will understand when you get older, my dear," he said, putting on one of his most grandfatherly smiles. "In any case, it's poor manners to insult someone in her presence." At that, apparently from out of thin air, La Renardette appeared, giving us all a black smile.

"The bessst of luck to you," she said. "I'm sure your pickles are quite finnne." Her voice sounded as slithery as a slimy serpent's.

"Will you join us for lunch?" said my grandfather, looking at me. "Pierre is invited too, of course."

"I'd rather eat dust," I said bitterly. I took Pierre's hand and stormed off down the steps.

"It is unwise to be at odds with your grandfather," he called after us as we walked away. "I cannot fathom why you choose to stick with a strange boy instead of your own flesh and blood. You know what they say—blood is thicker than water!"

When we were out of earshot, I crumpled down on a street corner. Pierre sat down beside me.

"It's no good," I said. "After this contest is over, I'll just have to go home and live with that—that monster."

"Hey, Aurore, you don't have to tell me, but how did you end up living with him? What happened to your parents?"

I'm not usually this abrupt, but my family history is a bit of a can of worms. "It's a long story, Pierre, and I'd prefer not to get into it right now." We both stared ahead. "Maybe I'll tell you someday," I said more quietly. "Anyhow, the ending of the story is that my grandfather is the only relative I now have. And however terrible he is, I guess I'm stuck with him."

"Why don't you come and live with us?" said Pierre.

"You really mean that?" I looked up with an expression of hope.

"Hey," said Pierre, "it's okay with me. And I'm sure I can convince my family. They'll get used to you." Thanks, Pierre. You really know how to give a compliment.

"Get *used* to me?"

Pierre poked me in the ribs. "Just kidding, Aurore—I got you there, didn't I?" Was this the same Pierre I knew? It was the first time I'd heard him play a joke like that. I shook my head.

The contestants were invited to see the final judging at three o'clock, so we had some time to ourselves. We roamed the streets of Bern for a while. We hadn't had anything to eat since the morning, so we stopped at a small pizza shop for a late lunch. As we ate, I looked around at the other tables. Funnily enough, I noticed a few other children our age, all eating pizza. They seemed to be in pairs, like us. A boy and a girl at each table. One pair was speaking in what sounded like Polish. Another boy and girl behind us were conversing in Chinese or some other Far Eastern language.

As we left the shop, I noticed yet another boy and girl pair who were talking in loud American accents.

"What are you two doing here in Bern?" I asked them in my somewhat accented English (I'll get a coach before starring in the movie—don't worry).

"Oh, we've entered into that pickle contest," said the girl. "And by golly we're going to win it!"

We'll see about that, I thought. Pierre and the boy just stared at each other oddly.

Finally, at two thirty, we headed back toward Graubünden Hall.

As we walked up the steps and into the hall, we were joined by several other contestants. Some of them were boys and girls I had seen at the pizza shop. Others were adult pairs, generally an old man and a younger woman, also speaking in various languages and dressed to match their countries of origin. *There's something unusual about this,* I thought.

We all shuffled into the wide hall. There were hundreds of chairs, and Pierre and I made our way close to the front. At the very front of the hall was a sort of stage. On the dais was a long table, behind which the three judges sat. The judges had their names on white place cards in front of them. On the table were several labeled jars of pickles. I tried to see if our jar was among them, but I wasn't close enough to tell.

I looked at the place cards, reading them off to Pierre in a hushed voice:

"Professor Sluughofter of Germany, Dr. Nodsttoppersonn of Norway, and Geveret Chutzpadickerstein of Israel . . ."

I noticed a girl a couple of seats to my left doing the same thing in what sounded like a Japanese accent.

"Where are you two from?" I asked her.

"I'm from a village outside Kyoto," she said brightly. "My name is Akira and this is Piyaro." I shook hands with Akira, and Pierre regarded Piyaro curiously.

As I looked between Piyaro and Pierre, I noticed that while Piyaro was Japanese and Pierre French, there was a certain similarity in their features. Akira, too, was looking at me closely.

"You came all the way here for the pickle contest?" I said to Akira. "Wow."

Piyaro spoke up. "My family's land is about to be bought out by a rich landowner. This pickle contest is our only chance to save it."

Before Pierre could answer, Piyaro gave a quick look behind us. "Do you see that man over there?" He jerked his head toward an aging Japanese gentleman, who was sitting beside a sleek but severe-looking young woman. "That's Akira's great-uncle,

Zakuru, but he's not very great. He wants to stop us from winning the contest. He tried to sabotage our boat, and we barely made it here with our lives."

"Interesting . . . ," I murmured. So . . . a boy and a girl on a quest to save their farm by winning a pickle contest. Now where had I heard that one before? Yes, there was certainly something very strange about all of this. Pierre felt it as well. But we had a competition to win, and I'm afraid to say that to this day, we still haven't gotten to the bottom of it.

Just then I noticed my own grandfather enter the hall, flanked by La Renardette. He sat down beside Zakuru, and soon the two of them started into an animated discussion (probably something to do with weaponry or deception, I guessed). La Renardette was glowering at Zakuru's companion (who was glowering back), and she held on to my grandfather's arm possessively.

"Attention, all contestants," said a voice. I looked up. It was the same man to whom we had given our pickles at the booth. He was standing on the stage with a microphone.

"Welcome to the Picklelympics!" he said loudly. There was applause. He continued.

"This is the contest for the best pickle of the

decade! For those of you who have not met me, my name is Rutger Jesselhoff, and I am the humble mayor of this fine town. I am happy to see all of you here." More loud applause from the audience. I clapped; Pierre just watched.

"Before we begin the proceedings, I want to unveil the centerpiece of this competition, a pickle exhibit designed by our very own picklemaster, Tinsel Troovinger."

At this, a youngish man with a quick step approached the stage. He had a quaint top hat on his head, and looked somewhat like a magician. He walked behind the stage and unlocked a partition on the wall. With the help of two other assistants, the partition was moved aside, revealing a very large display covered in a white sheet.

"Ladies and gentlemen, I present to you—the Tinsel Pickler!"

Tinsel yanked off the sheet to reveal an enormous vat, nearly as tall as the ceiling. Attached to its sides were large glass containers, each with various ingredients for making pickles.

"Watch!" cried Tinsel enthusiastically as he pulled a large wooden lever on the front of his pickler. As he did this, gas flames leaped up below the vat, and several of the glass containers moved up and over it in a circular motion, sprinkling ingredients inside the vat with precision. The crowd oohed and ahhed in appreciation. Tinsel bowed. There was enthusiastic applause. I regarded the vat with an inexplicable sense of apprehension. Pierre, too, was staring at it.

"And now for the main event of this competition," said Jesselhoff. "Our esteemed judges have spent the last two hours tasting pickles from all over the world—your pickles. And I have been told that all of you—at least almost all of you—should be extremely proud of yourselves for doing an excellent job."

"But since this is a competition for the *best* pickle, our judges had to be picky." Here there was some nervous laughter from the audience.

"They have selected the best five contestants from hundreds of entries and will be presently choosing our winners.

"As you know, the gold medal prize is worth $100,000. The second- and third-prize entries win $20,000 each.

"Before I announce the finalists, allow me to introduce our esteemed judges:

"Professor Sluughofter of Germany holds an advanced degree in Picklometry, the science of pickles and pickling. He is the director of the Berlin Institute for the Advancement of Pickles, and, I am told, his custom is to eat . . . only pickles." Professor Sluughofter, a tall and stern-looking man in his late fifties, rose and bowed. There was scattered applause.

"Dr. Nodsttoppersonn of Norway has studied the bacteria that grow on pickles for the last fifty years. In his very own greenhouse in Oslo, he is trying to grow a special kind of bacteria that could produce pickles that don't need to be refrigerated—ever." There was thunderous applause from the audience. Clearly, this was something they would appreciate. Doctor Nodsttoppersonn bowed. He was a short fat man with a bald head but a fiery red beard.

"Last but not least . . ."

"I can introduce myself, thank you very much," said Geveret Chutzpadickerstein of Israel, a tiny wisp of a woman, getting up and taking the microphone from Jesselhoff.

"You don't know from pickles," she said as the microphone buzzed with interference. Several people put their fingers in their ears. "You don't know from pickles," she repeated loudly. "I have been making pickles for my children and grand-children for longer than most of you have been alive," she said. "And let me tell you something— you don't know from pickles until you've been to my kitchen. I can tell you secrets about pickles that you have never dreamed. Do any of you know how to make a pickle with hummus?" The stunned crowd was speechless. "Anybody? Any-body? I didn't think so. After this contest is over, I invite all of you to my house, and I will show you how it's really done. Thank you." Some of the crowd clapped; others shook their heads in dismay.

"Thank you, Geveret Chutzpadickerstein," said Jesselhoff, happy to have the microphone back.

"And now, for our five finalists."

I was sitting on the edge of my seat, biting my nails. Pierre was just sitting. I couldn't tell if he was excited or not.

"From Poland—Trotsk Tumblers, entered by Auren Britz and Piotre Brakow." The Polish chil-dren cheered.

"From France—Les Cornichons Borsht, entered

by Zacharie Borsht." I watched a thin smile appear on my grandfather's face.

"From America—Schultz's Kosher Dill, entered by Anna Bornstein and Paul Brockovitz." Anna gave a hoot of joy. Paul just smiled.

"From Japan—Picosan, entered by Akira Zakuru and Piyaro Zakamato." The Japanese pair stood up and bowed. Akira's uncle, Zakuru, scowled.

I held my breath—there was only one entry left.

"And finally, from France—Cornichons La Bouche, entered by Aurore Borsht and Pierre La Bouche." I held on to Pierre's hand and squeezed. We were finalists!

"That's impossible," said my grandfather, raising his voice and standing up. "La Bouche pickles are disgusting. They're hardly pickles at all."

"Sir, sir," said Jesselhoff, "I request that you sit down, or I will have to disqualify you. I assure you that our selection process is meticulous."

My grandfather sat down slowly, and his evil grin gave way to a look of dismay. Clearly he believed that we had entered La Renardette's fake and revolting pickles. I saw the realization dawn on him.

He and La Renardette began arguing fiercely.

"But I thought you said La Bouche's pickles were destroyed!" I heard him say.

"They were!" said La Renardette.

My grandfather's face turned red. "Leave me," he said to her. "You're—you're fired."

La Renardette's eyes blazed. "You're firing me?" she said.

"That's right," said my grandfather.

"Well, you can't fire me—I quit!" Suddenly, a green cloud of smoke plumed about them. Several people coughed. When the smoke dispersed, La Renardette was nowhere to be seen.

"And good riddance," muttered my grandfather, sitting down again.

"And now," said Jesselhoff, "if there are no further interruptions, the judges will each taste the five finalists' entries."

The judges were now passed five lone pickles. Each pickle was on a porcelain plate that had the name of the contestant on it. The hall was silent in anticipation.

I watched Geveret Chutzpadickerstein nibble on one pickle, make a sour face, then nibble on another and make an even sourer face. *I hope that's not our pickle,* I thought to myself.

Finally, the nail-biting moments were over, and Jesselhoff collected the votes. He approached the microphone.

"I'm happy to announce that we have our winners," he said, beaming.

I almost couldn't take the suspense. Pierre blinked.

"In third place, winning our bronze medal—Schultz's Kosher Dill, entered by Anna Bornstein and Paul Brockovitz!"

Anna went wild and hugged just about everyone in her row. Paul maintained a serene demeanor, but I could see that he was glad.

"In second place, winning our silver medal—Trotsk Tumblers, entered by Auren Britz and Piotre Brakow!"

The Polish team danced a polka, and the crowd applauded them.

The applause died down. Jesselhoff cleared his throat.

Everyone in the hall held their breath.

Please, thought Pierre. *Please.* I squeezed his hand.

"And finally, in first place, the winners of the contest, the gold medal recipients are . . . *Cornichons La Bouche by Aurora Borsht and Pierre La Bouche!*"

I screamed with delight, jumped up and down, and hugged Pierre wildly. We had won the competition! Pierre was grinning from ear to ear, and I think he hugged me back, but I was so happy I can't even remember—I spent the next few moments in a daze.

Our joy was not to last long.

"You haven't won anything," said a steely voice behind us. We turned. My grandfather ripped off his sunglasses, drew a gun from the folds of his trench coat, and glared at Pierre with his glass eyeball gleaming.

"Run!" I cried. Pierre ran. My grandfather ran after him, waving his weapon—it was the ion gun I had seen in his bedroom drawer. Over chairs, around the stage, and across the hall they raced, straight toward the Tinsel Pickler. Panicking members of the audience were running in all directions. I tried to go after my grandfather from behind, but the rioting crowd was blocking my way.

Pierre didn't know where to go. The giant vat of boiling brine was right before him. On one side was a ladder. He scrambled up it with my grandfather at his heels. "You get back here, boy! I'm not through with you yet!" my grandfather shouted. Pierre saw a thin cord of wire that connected one side of the vat to the other. Evidently, it was there to facilitate the movement of the glass ingredient containers. Above the wire were the containers themselves, hanging over the steaming brine. Pierre, in a last desperate move, began to tiptoe across the wire. He got about halfway when my grandfather reached the top of the vat.

"You think you're the only one with good balance?" he called to Pierre, and to my amazement, began to step out onto the wire as well. "I know that's the secret to making pickles. I have it, you have it, and my brother has it. It's balance, Pierre, balance. Too salty, too sour, too sweet—and they're no good. Only we know how to make them perfect."

"Your brother?" asked Pierre, balancing on the wire, as my grandfather tried to unbalance him with sudden shakes of his feet.

"That's right, nephew," said my grandfather coldly. "Henri La Bouche is my brother. La Bouche is just a nickname he got as a soldier. He's a Borsht, just like I am, just like you are."

"Then why do you want to ruin him?" asked Pierre.

"That farm you call your farm really should have belonged to me. I was the firstborn, but our father always favored Henri. He said I didn't have Henri's courage. On his deathbed, he wrote a note that the farm belonged to Henri. Well, he was wrong about one thing. I do have courage—courage to take back what is rightfully mine. And now you're the only one in my way . . ."

Pierre stared back at my grandfather. "You call this courage? Shooting your own nephew for—for a piece of land? You're not brave at all. I call you a coward."

Not exactly the wisest thing to say when you've got a gun pointed at you, but at least he had guts.

"Maybe you're right, Pierre," said my grandfather. "This isn't about courage. This is about justice. My justice. And this, I'm afraid, is where it all comes to an end. Good-bye, Pierre."

By this time, I had managed to reach the judge's stage. "Take this, bubeleh," said Geveret Chutzpadickerstein, handing me a lone pickle, "and let that show-off see what you're made of."

I stared at the pickle dumbfoundedly.

My grandfather gritted his teeth and prepared to fire. Pierre closed his eyes.

"No!" I shouted, hurling the pickle at my grandfather.

The pickle struck my grandfather squarely in his glass eye, knocking it out of its socket. At the same instant he squeezed the trigger. A hot burst of white light erupted from the ion gun and ripped through the air.

It seemed, impossibly, that I could see the glowing jet of ions traveling in slow motion, moving with brilliant swiftness and power just to the right of Pierre's right ear, grazing it, then smashing against the far wall with a scorching hiss. My pickle must have thrown off his aim by just that much. My grandfather was pushed off balance by the recoil of the shot. For a moment he teetered, and then, with a loud cry, he plummeted headfirst into the boiling mixture. Pierre, too, teetered. His delicate mind-energy balance had been disrupted by the ion burst's wave of force. It looked as if he were about to fall into the vat as well.

"Ahhhh," cried Pierre agonizingly as he lost his balance. He fell. I screamed. But he did not land—at the last second, a dark figure swooped down from a hidden place above the exhibit. She caught Pierre as he fell, and the two of them gracefully flew through the air, landing on the other side of the vat.

Pierre looked into the face of his savior—my mouth was agape—it was La Renardette!

CHAPTER 14

One Big, Happy Family?

Man overboard!" called the mayor of Bern. Several of his assistants climbed up and fished Borsht out of the pickle soup. They lifted him down the ladder and put him on a stretcher.

"Is he alive?" I asked as they carried him away.

"He's breathing," said Jesselhoff. "But it appears that he's been—pickled."

It was true. My grandfather's skin had turned a green picklish hue, and there were warts and spots all over his face. His expression had taken on a sort of pickly tinge.

"Can you hear me?" I asked him. He looked up with a distant gaze.

"Aurore," he murmured. "Why, Aurore, you've grown up into such a lovely girl," he said in a sweeter, older voice than I had ever heard him use. "I'm—I'm not sure what happened to me. Won't you come and visit me sometime?"

I couldn't believe it. It seemed that the pickling had affected not just his looks but his whole personality. He had turned into a wizened old grandfather, the way an old grandfather should be. My eyes followed him as he was carried off to be given medical attention.

La Renardette and Pierre had climbed down from the other side of the exhibit and approached me.

"Are you okay?" I asked Pierre.

"Yes, thanks to her," he said.

"Thank you for saving his life," I said to La Renardette.

"Don't mention it," she said to us. "You don't know how I met your grandfather. It's a long story. I used to be in a circus. I was married to a man— we were both tightrope walkers. There was an accident. At least, I always thought it was an accident.

After I saw what your grandfather tried to do to you, I'm not so sure anymore. I had to save Pierre to make up for the past . . ."

"What's your real name?" said Pierre.

"Pierre!" I scolded.

"No, it's okay," she said. "You can call me Suzanne. Not as glamorous as La Renardette, but it's more me."

"Pleased to meet you," I said.

Pierre and I shook Suzanne's hand and wished her the best of luck in her new life.

"I think I'll become a gymnastics teacher," she said as she waved good-bye to us.

Jesselhoff approached us with five cashier's checks, each for $20,000. "Here's your prize money," he said. "I would deposit this right away in one of our fine banks. You've earned every cent. Well done, and marvelous, marvelous pickles! Oh, I almost forgot, Pierre. For helping us reset our town clock, we have a special gift. A box of our finest Bernese chocolates!" He handed Pierre an exquisite-looking wooden box of chocolates. I could already see Pierre licking his lips.

"Here are your gold medals," said Jesselhoff, producing two fine-looking medals from a case.

We donned the medals and walked up to the stage with the other winners. Most of the crowd had returned after the excitement was over, and they cheered us loudly.

I noticed that Pierre was gazing at Piyaro, the Japanese contestant. Piyaro looked gloomy. He had not placed, and now his family's land was going to be sold. Pierre was fingering the checks uncomfortably. *Maybe I should do it,* he was thinking, *but what about my family? . . . Still . . .*

Suddenly Pierre jumped down from the stage and walked over to Piyaro. He handed him one of the checks.

"This is for your family," he said.

"Twenty thousand dollars!" exclaimed Akira, examining the check. "We cannot accept this from you."

"I don't want you to lose your farm," said Pierre firmly. "Take it, it's yours."

Piyaro was speechless. It seemed he was close to tears.

"You are a generous young man," said a voice. We turned. It was Zakuru.

"What more do you want from us?" said Akira bitterly.

"I have seen an act of great kindness," said Zakuru. "This boy has taught me a lesson. I have decided not to buy out your family's land. The land is yours to keep."

Piyaro and Akira couldn't believe their ears. Seconds later they were hugging Zakuru. The three were in tears. Zakuru's companion watched from the side. It was hard to tell what she was thinking.

Piyaro turned to Pierre and gave back the check. "I thank you for your generosity, Pierre-san, but it is now not necessary. We are going home."

"So are you two, I figure," said a twangy Texas accent. We looked up and saw Captain John Klinger of the U.S. paratroopers approaching us. "Care for a lift to the La Bouche farm?" he said.

Pierre and I grinned.

Hours later, as we flew over the Swiss hill country, and then back to my French homeland in Klinger's plane, I mulled over what had happened. That ion burst had disrupted Pierre's fine balance. That was what had thrown him off the wire. But was he still average, predictable Pierre? I looked at him closely as he stared out the window. When had he become so unusually generous, caring enough to give a complete stranger part of the prize money that his family needed so badly? Had the ion burst unbalanced him in that way too? Somehow I didn't think so. Pierre will always be Pierre. But maybe we all change as we drift through our lives.

Had I changed from our adventure? Me? The Great Aurore? Impossible.

"Pierre!" cried Henri La Bouche as we got out of the plane and jogged toward the farmhouse.

The rest of the La Bouche family had also gathered around. There were hugs and kisses all over.

"We heard the results on the radio," said Frieda. "Amazing. You did it. I'm so proud of you, Pierre!"

"Here is the prize money," said Pierre, handing Henri the five checks. "I guess we can stay on the farm now, Grandfather." Henri beamed from ear to ear, then kissed Pierre on both cheeks. "Yes, we can, Pierre," he said, still glowing.

"And who is this?" asked Chantal curiously.

"Chantal," said Pierre, "this is your cousin, Aurore—"

"La Bouche," I said quickly. The others, especially Henri, looked at me quizzically. "It's a long story," I explained. "But I'm a great storyteller!"

Klinger shook hands with Henri. He was clearly in awe.

"I have the utmost respect for you, sir," he said. "You saved my father's life."

"Thank you for helping my grandson," said Henri.

"It was my pleasure, sir. Why, I think he's a chip off the old block. And *I* should be thanking *him*." Here Klinger slapped Pierre on the back. "He's quite a pilot! I had a devil of a time tracking down my plane in the Alps, but he landed it like a true expert. And he and his friend rescued my injured pilot too. You should be proud of him."

"I am," said Henri.

Klinger shook hands with us, gave Pierre another mighty slap on the back, and took off in his plane. We all waved good-bye.

As we walked toward the farm hand in hand, I whispered to Pierre, "Are you going to tell your grandfather that it was your pickles and not his that won the contest?"

Pierre looked ahead, thinking, *Should I tell him?*

But how will he feel when he finds out they weren't his pickles?

"Tell us everything," said Henri as we all sat in the La Bouche kitchen.

"Do you want the long version or the short one?" asked Pierre, smiling at me. Everyone laughed.

We talked late into the night. When I described our duel in the catacombs and our brush with François, Jo Jo jumped up and down with glee. "He was so funny, that François," said Jo Jo. "I knew he was a bandit, but he turned all mushy when I saved his daughter."

Pierre decided to skip our little detour in the Alps—for now. There were too many delicate issues involved.

"And do you know, Chantal," I said, "you are very highly regarded at DERN—I mean CERN." Chantal gave a short smile and stifled a laugh.

"What I can't figure out," said Marc innocently, "is how you managed to go through so many adventures and still hold on to Grandfather's pickle jar."

"Oh, I had help," said Pierre, looking at me.

Henri watched us and smiled. But there was a touch of sadness in his face. I believe he was starting to guess about the parts of the story we had left out.

Later, much later, after everyone had gone to bed, Henri came upstairs to say good night to Pierre.

From the open door in the next room, as I lay there on my bed, I could just overhear it.

Henri knelt by Pierre's bed and kissed him on the forehead.

"You're a real hero," said Pierre. "I never knew about what you did in the war."

"Oh, that?" said Henri. "That was nothing. Anyone could have done that. Now what you did . . ."

"What did I do?" said Pierre. "I just took a jar of pickles to the contest. There's nothing heroic about that."

"That depends on whose jar of pickles you took," said Henri.

Pierre was silent. *He knows.*

"That's okay, Pierre. I do know. I know it wasn't my pickles that won the contest. It was yours."

"No, Grandfather—"

"Pierre, the truth is always better—more difficult, but better. I am proud of you. So very proud. I always knew you could be the man I see you are becoming. I am happy that it turned out this way."

"Grandpa, there's something else I didn't tell you. In the Alps, after we landed the plane, there's somebody we met. She—"

"Yes, Pierre, I know," said Henri quickly. "There are so many things we still must discuss. But I think you have told me enough for tonight. Tomorrow is a new day."

I guess he's not ready for that yet, Pierre thought. *But someday . . .* He sighed, and let his head fall back on his pillow.

"I love you, Grandfather. Good night," he said, closing his eyes. And then, as he drifted off to sleep and Henri watched his peaceful face, Henri sang Pierre a lullaby. I had heard the words before:

Little baby, my sweet baby,
You are resting in my arms,
The day is gone,
The night has come,
And now it's time to sleep,
While the stars shining bright,

Are dancing overhead
It is you, dearest boy, I will tuck into bed.

🫙

Would Henri ever be reunited with Rochelle? I don't know. Perhaps that is for another adventure. This one is ending, and others always come.

The story is almost wound up now, and there's not much else left to tell. Using the prize money, Henri was able to pay off his creditors and hold on to the farm. The La Bouches were happy to take me in permanently, and Pierre and I soon became part of the pickling process. It turned out that Pierre had not lost his perfect balance in the shooting, and he was as good as ever at making pickles. With our help, the farm began to prosper again.

I called my grandfather a few weeks later to see how he was doing. He had moved to a seniors' apartment complex in Paris and was enjoying his new life. I can't fathom how that dunk in the steaming brine had managed to change him so drastically from an evil plotter into a sweet old man, but it was as if I were speaking to a different person. I guess pickles are like that. They're cucumbers, but then again, are they? After they get soaked in that brine, they've changed into something else entirely.

Speaking of pickles, I forgot to mention: the mayor of Bern gave us three from Pierre's winning jar. Not wanting to stir up family jealousy, we ate two of them privately, on a quiet afternoon at the edge of the farm. They were splendiferously pickli-cious and bursting with unique cosmopolitan fla-vorosity! (How's that for a review?) The third we put into a small glass container, which we sealed with wax. We buried it under a special tree not far from the farmhouse. Eventually it will go bad, start growing mold, and then it will really look interest-ing for whoever digs it up.

And soon I'll be famous, just like I said in the beginning. But after I'm done starring in the movie that's about this story, I don't think I'll move to America. Well, not yet at any rate. No, the Great Aurore's place right now is here, with Pierre and his family, farming cornichons, making the best pickles in the world, and just perhaps having an adventure or two, or four . . . well, at least some of the time.

That about does it. Have I told you the best

story you have heard all year? Did I lie? Do you believe me? There are many things in life that are impossible, but they happen every day.

Now look at me. The Great Aurore, the brilliant storyteller, her story done, and now she doesn't know how to say good-bye to you. Well, here goes— my friend, thank you for sticking with me and Pierre. And Pierre, if you are reading these lines, sorry for making so much fun of you—it was too much fun not to.

Oh, dear, this is really the end. Good-bye! Good-bye! Farewell!

Did I mention there is a potato chip contest this fall?

Do you believe me? Oh, what a pickle.

But a good one.

See you there!

Bye, now, and really good-bye!

Yours forever,

The Great Aurore

P.S. The End

Geveret Chutzpadickerstein's Homemade Pickles

Bubeleh, yes, you—come into my kitchen. I told you that you don't know from pickles. Well, I know from pickles. Let me show you how it's done. Here is what you'll need:

10 small, firm, fresh cucumbers, scrubbed clean
4 cloves of garlic
2 sprigs of dill (stems and heads)
1 cup coarse pickling salt (that's the thick kind)
3 cups white vinegar
15 cups water
A big, sealable glass jar or Mason jar
A large metal pot
Metal tongs

Now listen to what I say carefully, and watch that you don't burn your fingers! Are you listening?

1. Make sure the pot and the jar are very clean.

2. Fill the pot with water and bring it to a boil.

3. Holding the jar with metal tongs, dunk it in the pot and leave underwater for a minute, to kill all the nasty germs.

4. Use the tongs to take the jar out of the pot.

5. Chop up the garlic.

6. Put the cucumbers, garlic, and dill into the jar.

7. Change the water in the pot.

8. Add the salt and vinegar to the water. Now it's called brine.

9. Bring the brine in the pot to a simmer.

10. Carefully pour the brine into the jar, filling it to the very top.

11. Seal the jar, but not too tightly.

12. Put the jar on a windowsill where it's sunny. Wait for two weeks.

13. After two weeks are up, open the jar, top it up with some more brine, and close it again.

14. Put the jar in the fridge and wait a day.

15. Take the jar out of the fridge and open it.

16. Take a pickle out.

17. Dip the pickle in hummus.

18. Put the pickle in your mouth.

19. Chew. Swallow.

20. Smile.

Acknowledgments

This story began with an old man's face on a raisin container. His bulging cheeks and the farm in the background made me think of Grandfather Henri La Bouche. But pickles were in the fridge and it was snack time so . . . And now it's hard to believe Aurore isn't as real as you or I. Whatever the case, I wish her the best of success in her cinematic endeavors!

Now to thanks—thank G-d for giving me the strength to write this book and keep up being a decent dad at the same time. I can only begin to thank my family for sticking by me as I went on and on about the La Bouches. Elana Roth, my fantastic agent, deserves special thanks for believing in me. So does my wonderful editor, Caroline Abbey, for taking Pierre and Aurore to the next level. Thanks, thanks, thanks to my loyal critics: the young and young-at-heart of the Stutz, Weil, Amsel, Sapir, Shefer, Amishav, and Kellerstein families. And to Grandma Jenny for minding my French. You guys rock.